WIPEOUT!
&
HANGING TEN
IN PARIS

Two Surfing Detective Mysteries

Other Surfing Detective books
by Chip Hughes

MURDER ON MOLOKA'I

KULA

SURFING DETECTIVE

CONFIDENTIAL INVESTIGATIONS : ALL ISLANDS

WIPEOUT!

&

HANGING TEN IN PARIS

Two Surfing Detective Mysteries

CHIP HUGHES

SLATE RIDGE PRESS

Slate Ridge Press

P.O. Box 1886
Kailua, HI 96734
slateridgepress@hawaii.rr.com

ISBN: 098294442X
ISBN 13: 978-0-9829444-2-4

Wipeout! © Chip Hughes 2007
Slate Ridge Press edition © 2012

Hanging Ten in Paris © Chip Hughes 2012

WIPEOUT!

A Surfing Detective Mystery

For Mark Foo, Todd Chesser,
Donny Solomon, Malik Joyeux,
and other big wave riders
who have lost their lives
in the pursuit.

"If you want to experience the ultimate thrill,
you have to be willing to pay the ultimate price."

—*Big-wave rider Mark Foo*

Foreword

By Big-Wave Pioneer Fred Van Dyke

Wipeout! will grasp you from the very beginning. No details have been overlooked. The characters, the events are woven together in an inextricable mystery that unfolds slowly, and it is not until the very end that you realize what has taken place. There is really no second guessing the author. Many times when you are expecting one thing to happen, the opposite occurs.

I am a big-wave surfing legend who lived thirty years adjacent to the famous Pipeline break, having the experience of nearly losing my home on a number of occasions to the huge waves that sweep the beach during winter months. I have wiped out at Waimea and all the other big-wave breaks on Oʻahu. I passed into the other world on a wipeout, but it was not my time to lose my life. I feel deeply what Chip writes and describes.

As I was reading, I totally became a part of the narrative. The scenes out at Waimea Bay happen similarly. The people who live on the North Shore are depicted in a real fashion. I have lost friends to the Waimea ferociousness—closest to me was Mark Foo, who handled Waimea beautifully but lost his life at Mavericks.

Chip was able to fully wrap me into the story by this authenticity of description. I could feel the dry throat, the anxiety of waiting for a closeout set on the horizon, the flushed face, being caught in the riptide and washed seaward after losing your board.

The relationship you feel between the board and yourself is an important part of surfing and Chip caught that, nearly making the board seem like a friend or an extension of body and mind.

Whether you're a surfer, a mystery lover, or both, *Wipeout!* is a read I think you will enjoy.

Fred Van Dyke
April 2006

Acknowledgments

Many thanks once again to my wife, Charlene, whose inspiration guides my writing and my life, to my mother, Kathryn Cooley Hughes, for her unflagging support, and to Stu Hilt for sharing his nearly fifty years' experience as a Honolulu P.I.

Mahalo to big-wave legend Fred Van Dyke for his generous foreword; to my writing group—LaRene Despain, Sue Cowing, and Felix Smith; to Les Peetz, Lorna Hershinow, Kuʻualoha Hoʻomanawanui, Ian MacMillan, Steven Goldsberry, and Rodney Morales; and to my invaluable editor, Kirsten Whatley.

one

"Are you the Surfing Detective?" she asked in a voice as soft as trade winds whispering in bamboo.

"Yes ..." I wondered if this was yet another crank call.

"Good, because you're the only one who can help."

That got my attention.

She kept details to a minimum, then made an appointment and promised an advance.

A few mornings later I waited for her in a red vinyl booth at the second-floor Denny's in Waikīkī. The aroma of lattes and espressos wafting up from the Starbucks below made me wish I was down there on Kapahulu Avenue, or on my way to a morning surf session.

But she had chosen Denny's. She didn't say why. And she was late.

I sat there in my most flamboyant aloha shirt—*hula* dancers, Diamond Head, swaying coconut palms and, yes, surfers— watching the sun shimmer on glistening Kapi'olani Park and the damp, cocoa-colored sands of Waikīkī Beach. The campy aloha shirt was to help her recognize me, along with the mostly true description of myself I had given: sun-bleached brown hair, six feet even (a stretch), and a perpetual tan from surfing. I didn't mention my age, thirty-four, nor did I claim Hawaiian ancestry. Though my name, Kai, means "sea" and though I was *hānaied,* or adopted, by a Hawaiian family when I was eight, my Cooke ancestors were about as New England as you can get. Anyway, all my client seemed to care about was that I was both a surfer *and* a detective.

By 10:15 most evidence of the morning showers had vanished, but the pavement on Kapahulu still ran blacker than usual to the beach. There were few surfers out today. This morning's gloomy grey canopy—coupled with small surf on the South Shore—had kept all but the diehards at home. Most had gone up to the North Shore, where a huge winter swell was thundering in from storms in the North Pacific—off Japan, off China, off the Aleutian Islands, off who knows where in that immense, blue, fathomless ocean.

We'd had some enormous days in December and January. Twenty-five feet. Thirty feet. February figured to bring more really big ones.

Today was Monday, February 3. I stared through the steam swirling up from my coffee. If I were a smoker, I would have lit up about now. Instead, from the pocket of my aloha shirt, behind a swaying palm, I slipped a sweet *li hing mui* crack seed onto my tongue and instantly the sweet-sour plum pit exploded with pungent flavor.

Glancing up I saw a woman who was very *hāpai,* very pregnant, at the entrance. She caught my eye and made her way toward me. I ditched the crack seed in my napkin.

"Summer?" I stood and clasped her trembling hand and breathed in the flowery scent of her perfume. She nodded as she slipped her hand from mine and edged slowly into the booth.

"Want some coffee?" I noticed her eyes were violet—not blue, but intensely violet like orchids. Then I gazed at her protruding tummy. "Uh ... orange juice? Milk?"

"Nothing, thank you," she replied in that whispering voice I'd heard earlier on the phone. I leaned toward her so I wouldn't miss a word.

Summer's hair was blonde, wheat blonde, turned under in the golden roll of a pageboy. She had a cute cheerleader nose and a dimple in her chin. Back in California, she would have been that knockout in high school every guy had a crush on at least once.

"How difficult this must be for you," I said. "I'm very sorry about your husband."

She tried for a smile that didn't even reach the corners of her mouth. Her delicate hands were folded neatly on the tabletop. Her violet eyes looked misty.

"You said on the phone you wanted me to look into his death?"

She nodded.

"It happened in December at Waimea Bay?" I prompted.

"Yes, on the day before Christmas at sunset, almost Christmas eve."

"Did you see him wipe out?" I recalled the incident from news coverage. Corky McDahl had been pounded by a succession of twenty-foot waves and not seen again.

"No." She glanced down at her tummy. "We thought with the baby due soon and all ..."

"So you stayed behind in …where is it you live again in California?"

"Newport Beach."

"And you didn't mind staying home while he surfed in Hawai'i?"

"I'm very independent. So was Corky." She pulled from her purse a snapshot and handed it to me. "My husband." She introduced him as if he were still alive and sitting with us in the booth.

I glanced at the photo of a deeply tanned man in his middle twenties. Under a thatch of straw yellow curls, green eyes dominated. Mirrored sunglasses, the expensive kind some surfers wear, hung from a cord around his neck. His adolescent smile turned downward on one side, revealing a hint of attitude. He looked agitated, like a guy about to throw a punch.

"Corky took out a two-hundred-thousand-dollar life insurance policy before his trip," Summer said. "The time lapse clause, or whatever they call it, matured just a few days before his accident, but the insurance company hasn't paid. Mr. Gold, the adjuster, is very apologetic."

"Surfers do unfortunately sometimes disappear. Your Mr. Gold must know that."

"Oh, he does. It's not just the short time the policy was in effect. Mr. Gold says Corky's case raises several red flags."

"What red flags?"

"Corky withdrew all our savings before he left," she said matter-of-factly.

"Did he tell you he was going to clean out the account?"

"No, not at the time. But he probably needed the money for his trip." She seemed unconcerned by an action some spouses might consider treacherous and disloyal.

"What else?"

"Corky charged our credit cards over the limit. A few charges came through even after he died."

"The card could have been stolen," I conjectured, "or the purchases posted late."

"Well, we have low spending limits, so it's no surprise he went over them. Another thing," Summer went on, "Mr. Gold asked me why Corky would have been seen driving a BMW convertible—an expensive new model."

"What did you tell him?"

"I said Corky didn't own a BMW. We couldn't afford one. But he had an auto detailing business in California. He may have earned extra money in Hawai'i by working on that BMW, and just took it for a ride."

The red flags were adding up. "Anything else?"

She shook her head. "Corky always wanted to be a big name surfer—a sponsored surfer—and he looked at his trips here as investments in his career—and in our future. He dreamed that someday, somehow, a sponsor would discover him. He even changed his name from Charles to Corky after a legendary California surfer…"

"Corky Carroll?"

"Yes, I believe that's the one. Corky… er, Charles … talked about his idol constantly, though he never actually met him."

I caught myself gazing at her again. I was thinking about her baby. If she were my wife, and in the last months of her pregnancy, would I abandon her to ride the world's biggest, most dangerous waves? Maybe Corky didn't want to be a father after all. Maybe he preferred to go out in a blaze of glory, rather than face his parental responsibilities.

"Summer, I have to ask you this." I hated to say it out loud. "Do you know any reason why your husband would fake his own death?"

She shook her head. "It wasn't like him to do something so desperate."

"Not even to defraud the insurance company of two hundred thousand dollars?"

"Not my Corky."

The waitress came by and refilled my coffee. "Would you like anything?" I asked Summer again.

"Nothing, thanks," she said.

"It won't be easy to prove your husband died." I tried to be realistic with her. "When surfers disappear, a shredded wet suit or torn board shorts may be all that turns up. Some vanish without a trace."

She didn't respond, but kept looking at me hopefully.

"'Course Waimea on a big day is like a huge outdoor arena, with hundreds of onlookers and photographers, so we may come up with something. A bobbing surfer might have been spotted, though maybe not after sunset when your husband wiped out. But even if I find evidence of your husband's …"—I groped for words—"evidence of your husband, I can't guarantee the insurance company will accept it as proof."

Summer's determined look suggested she wasn't fazed by what I'd said.

"How soon can you start?"

"Right away. But about the retainer…" I reminded her of her promise. "In a case like this confined to O'ahu, five hundred would be OK for starters."

She reached into her purse and pulled out a handful of crumpled green bills—all Ben Franklins—setting them on the table. There must have been a dozen hundreds easily, all wadded up and wrinkled.

I separated out five crumpled notes and slid the others across the table to her.

"I wish you would take them all, so I don't have to make another trip here." She slid the bills back my way. "I trust you'll return what you don't use."

I decided not to argue with her. I gathered up all that green and shoved it behind the swaying palm on the pocket of my aloha shirt.

"Where are you staying?" I asked, in a lighter mood now. "Can I give you a lift?"

She pulled a paper from her purse and handed it to me. The phone number on it began with 739-. *Kāhala? Ritzy Kāhala?*

"The Kāhala Resort?" I asked. "That's a posh hotel."

"No, a private home," she said. "You can call me there."

"You have friends in Kāhala?"

She nodded but didn't explain. As she struggled up from the table, I handed her my card. "I'll phone you as soon as I have anything to report."

Summer glanced at the longboard rider on the sand-toned card and slipped it into her purse.

My eyes returned to her bulging middle. "When is your baby due?"

"Early March—so the doctors say." Summer made a cute smirk that almost turned into a smile. "They're never right, you know. My mother tells me I came three weeks early."

"Three weeks early for your baby would mean just a few days from now…"

Summer shrugged. "The baby will wait until you find evidence of my Corky." Her confidence worried me.

She started to walk away. Before she got out of earshot I couldn't help saying, only half joking, "Delivering babies is not in my standard contract."

She turned around, shrugged again, and then duck-stepped past rows of mostly empty booths and out the door. A few minutes later, on the street below, I saw Summer climb awkwardly into a hearse-black Mercedes sedan. A door closed and she disappeared behind darkly tinted glass. The Mercedes turned toward Diamond Head and soon vanished.

Later, when disentangling the green bills Summer had left behind, I counted not twelve, but sixteen. Sixteen hundred dollars. *In cash.* More than I would need, no doubt, since this case was most likely going nowhere.

Better than a month had passed since Corky wiped out. If he had died in the huge surf, by now his bones would be licked clean, if any bones remained at all. I could try to find his board and track down his credit card purchases and maybe even locate the BMW he was allegedly seen driving. But evidence of his body? No way.

Unless, of course, Corky had pulled off one of the most daring skip traces in recorded history. But to play dead in Waimea's massive winter surf would have amounted to suicide. Twenty-foot waves are not make-believe. That Corky would go to such lengths simply to escape paternal responsibilities seemed unlikely—unless he and Summer together were trying to defraud the insurance company to the tune of two hundred grand.

If this was their game, the pregnant blonde was well coached—her trembling hands, her misty eyes. But her story didn't match her bankroll. If Corky had left her broke, how was

Summer underwriting her trip to Hawai'i? And what about her friends with the Kāhala phone number and black Mercedes?

I pocketed the cash again and, despite my qualms, found myself sympathizing with the violet-eyed widow.

Whatevahs. I had a case. Or it had me.

two

Located on Maunakea Street above Fujiyama's Lei Shop, my office is about the size and sturdiness of a Cracker Jack box. It boasts one window overlooking the bustle and varied aromas and questionable charm of the storied old ramshackle street. Just one block down, amidst the color and ambience of Chinatown, is notorious Hotel Street. Once the province of pimps, prostitutes, porno palaces, and flop houses, these days you're more likely to find art galleries and ethnic eateries.

I pulled open the bottom drawer of my battleship grey filing cabinet, on which sits a tarnished surf-rider trophy: Classic Longboard . . . Mākaha . . . Third Place. *My faded glory.* Way in the back of the musty bottom drawer where I store personal files, I reached for a manila folder of news clippings labeled Big-Wave Wipeouts.

The first story my eyes fell on eulogized Tahiti surfer Malik Joyeux who died at Banzai Pipeline in December 2005. The lip of a powerful wave had hit him dead on, broken his board in half, and ripped off the leash. Joyeux was found under water, about two hundred yards from where he had wiped out. The treacherous Banzai riptide had carried him away.

The next clipping recalled the drowning of Todd Chesser near Waimea Bay in February 1997. A faded photo showed Chesser—glistening shaved head and seal black wetsuit—shooting a mammoth green tube during the filming of *In God's Hands.* Another photo pictured the memorial service for the wave rider at Ali'i Beach Park in Hale'iwa, attended by hundreds of fellow surfers and family and friends.

Next came a raggedly torn and yellowed *Star-Bulletin* clipping about Mark Foo's wipeout in 1994 at Mavericks in Half Moon Bay near San Francisco. More stories about Foo's drowning lay beneath this clipping and some glossy magazine spreads commemorating his life.

Where did I put that one about Corky? I thumbed through the folder crammed with clippings. Who knows how I got started collecting such sensational and morbid stories? I also collect accounts of surfers attacked by sharks, since it happened to me. But the shark-bite pieces have their own separate folder.

"'The Wave of His Life' Was His Last." There it was. The *Honolulu Advertiser,* December 25, Christmas day. And there was Corky's straw hair, intense eyes, and cocky smile.

The accompanying story told how Corky had wiped out at Waimea on Christmas Eve. The sun had set, but the huge waves kept cranking, enticing surfers to stay out in the crimson afterglow. The waves that got him were twenty feet—a two-story building. Though the irony of big wave tragedies is that typically the unfortunate surfer miraculously survives the biggest wave of the day, only to be pummeled to death by a smaller one.

Corky had just successfully ridden a monster of nearly thirty feet. "He died with a smile on his face," proclaimed a fellow surfer. "He was grinning from ear to ear. Corky wished

me 'Merry Christmas' and then paddled out for another one."
The next wave would be his last. "It's the way he'd want to go,"
said the surfer. "Not die in a car wreck or slowly wither of old
age. He died happy. I'm glad for him."

The *Advertiser* continued: "The 27-year-old California
native could not catch the first wave of the next set and was
pounded back by three 20-footers that followed." A lifeguard
was quoted: "We figure the big waves pushed him deep
underwater and kept him there. His body may never be found.
It happens this way sometimes, unfortunately for loved ones
left behind."

Three twenty-footers thundering in. Like freight trains.
Caught in that boiling soup, tumbling head over heels and
struggling to hold his breath, he wouldn't have known which
way was up.

What must happen in white water twenty feet high? You
probably *whirl*. Like a feather in a gale, only not so gently. It
must feel more like the spin cycle of an industrial-strength
washer. Or being massaged by a hammer—*jackhammer*. Most
likely, Corky turned endlessly in the dark, exploding wave,
then was sucked out unconscious to sea in Waimea's powerful
riptide. What happened afterwards is anybody's guess.

According to another clipping, more than a month later
no trace of his body had been found. Not even a shred of his
wetsuit. The tiger sharks that roam these coastal waters—those
silent, steel-jawed killers—sometimes leave nothing behind.

The sole known remains of Corky McDahl was his
surfboard. The candy cane-striped board had drifted to shore,
evidently ripped by coral on its tumultuous ride. The battered
board shown in the *Advertiser* photo had no chunks missing, no
telltale saw-toothed crescents torn from its rails. I decided to

pay a visit to the Honolulu Police Department later that day—they'd have sharper photos than this newsprint image.

I glanced at my answering machine. The red light was flashing like a warning beacon, so I pressed Play.

"Kai? I missed you last night," said the shy, childlike voice. "Weren't we going to see that film?"

Leimomi. Just like her to sound not the least bit angry—just pondering if she had the wrong day or time. She had them right. I forgot. Again. I had promised to take her to a movie remake of *The Merry Widow* that critics touted as "spellbinding" and "hilariously funny." Some woman whose husband is barely in the grave takes up with another man and causes quite an uproar. It didn't interest me in the least. I would have preferred to see a new surfing documentary that was playing. Maybe that's why I forgot about Leimomi's film.

"Are we seeing *The Merry Widow* tonight?" Leimomi asked plaintively. "Not last night, but tonight?"

I imagined her waiting for me last night in her Punchbowl duplex after stringing *lei* all day in Mrs. Fujiyama's shop. Leimomi didn't even phone my apartment with her innocent, slightly hurt questions, but that's not her style. When she called my office the next morning expecting to find me in, I was sitting in a booth at Denny's in Waikīkī gazing into the violet eyes of a pregnant California blonde.

What I had done yesterday instead of showing up for my date with Leimomi was surf. I paddled out to my favorite spot in town, offshore of the Sheraton Waikīkī—the long, hollow, right-breaking walls of Populars. I rode waves until the mango orange sun slipped into the sea. Then in twilight I strolled back to my apartment—a studio penthouse on the forty-fifth floor of the Waikīkī Edgewater—and hopped into a long hot shower.

By seven, when I was supposed to be pulling into Leimomi's duplex, I was sipping a beer in front of the Triple Crown of Surfing recap on ESPN.

"Kai, I'm off today so I won't see you at work. Would you call me . . . please?" Leimomi's voice drifted from the answering machine. I sighed.

A second message contained the sardonic voice of my attorney friend, Tommy Woo: "Hey, Kai, how many piano players does it take to change a light bulb?"

Another doozy. The punch line included the names of keyboard legends Bill Evans, Keith Jarrett, and Yanni, and to my tone-deaf ear made absolutely no sense. Though he practiced law, Tommy's true passion was the jazz piano.

"How about dinner?" continued Tommy. "Got a gig on Tuesday, but Wednesday looks good. Same old place at seven?"

Same old place meant Ah Fook Chop Sui House on River Street in Chinatown, where the best thing on the menu was the prices. If Tommy and I have anything in common, it's being cheap.

I erased the messages and returned to my newspaper clipping on the unfortunate Corky McDahl. "The best wave of his life . . . The way he'd want to go . . . He died with a smile on his face . . ." It all sounded so convincing—such a purposeful, happy death. Not something you could easily fake. I scanned the not-yet-yellowed newsprint once again—then realized I was procrastinating. *Call Leimomi.* I picked up the phone and dialed. It rang three times, then her answering machine kicked in.

"Sorry about last night, Leimomi . . ."

As I began to sheepishly explain, there was a barely audible tap on my door.

"Be right with you!" I barked through the solid mahogany. "I'll take you to that film, Lei. How about tomorrow night?"

Tap. Tap. Tap. This time not so faint.

"Look, I'll have to call you back. A customer is knocking. We'll see that movie, I promise."

"Coming!" I reached for the knob and swung open the door. "Leimomi? What are you doing here?"

Startled into abruptness, I gazed down upon her. She stood barely five feet in sandals—waist-length brown hair, mocha-colored skin, eyes glistening like black pearls. She was a Kaua'i girl whose mixed Japanese, Chinese, and Filipino heritages blended together beautifully.

"You don't work today," I said, studying her innocent face for some clue. A simple black shift hanging on her slim frame revealed just a hint of the curves I knew were there. Her expression looked neither anxious nor angry, but bewildered.

"I wondered," she said in her quiet voice, "if anything was wrong."

"No, nothing is wrong. I'm sorry about last night. I know you wanted to see that movie."

"We can see it another time," she said almost apologetically, as if the missed date were *her* fault. I suddenly felt guiltier than if she had given me the verbal thrashing I deserved.

"I know we can see that movie another time," I uttered abjectly, "but today was your day off and all, and we had planned to spend some time together last night . . ."

"So you still love me then?" She peered into my eyes with those glistening pearls.

"Of course."

"And everything is all right between us?"

"Everything is fine."

"Good, because I worried last night . . . I worried that after all we've shared you really didn't love me."

"Why are you so worried?"

"We need to talk, Kai. But . . ." She hesitated.

"Is something wrong?" I was becoming curious.

"Tomorrow night would be better." She lowered her dark eyes. "OK?"

"OK," I agreed, though I didn't like to be left hanging.

"Kiss me, Kai." She puckered her plum red lips. So I did.

Leimomi then turned and glided down the dim hallway, past the offices of my fellow tenants: passport photographer, accountant, freelance editor, and psychic Madame Zenobia. Soon Leimomi disappeared down the orange shag stairs.

I gave her a few minutes to clear the building, imagining she might stop to chat with the other *lei* girls and with Mrs. Fujiyama. Then I grabbed my manila folder with the clippings and headed down the stairs.

As I walked through the shop, I glanced into the back room and saw Chastity and Joon stringing sweet-scented *pīkake*. Another *lei* girl, Blossom, sat nearby tying off a pale yellow plumeria *lei*. Passing the refrigerated cases displaying colorful strands of island flowers, I glimpsed Mrs. Fujiyama at the cash register, bone thin, steel haired, and, as always during business hours, wearing a courteous smile.

"Good morning, Mrs. Fujiyama," I said.

She glanced up at me over half glasses, her smile suddenly bending into a frown. "Good morning, Mr. Cooke."

Strange. Mrs. Fujiyama and I were on the most cordial of terms, though she was a stern mother hen hovering over her *lei* girls.

"Anything wrong, Mrs. Fujiyama?"

"Nothing wrong, Mr. Cooke," she replied in an expressionless tone that suggested otherwise.

I stepped from the flower shop onto Maunakea Street and headed for my parking garage. The sharp competing smells of kim chee, cappuccino, rancid garbage, and screw-cap wine reached my nose. As I turned in, I realized the silent wrath of my landlady was making me feel nearly as guilty as the apologetic behavior of my girlfriend.

three

Cruising toward HPD headquarters on Beretania Street, I spotted a black Mercedes in my rearview mirror. The car was behind three others, so I couldn't swear it was the same black Mercedes Summer had climbed into after our Denny's meeting. But I didn't doubt it either.

I kept my eye on the car as my Impala growled along, turning a few heads. My '69 Chevy is not your nondescript, front-wheel-drive, pale imitation Impala of today, but a genuine V-8, gas-guzzling, glitzy dream machine of the sixties. The real thing.

My surfboard rode beside me inside the teal cockpit, the nine-six's rounded, duckbill nose resting comfortably on the padded dash. That's the beauty of an outsized classic car like this—pop out the backseat and my longboard slides right in. I like to bring my board along even when I'm not heading for the surf. On the spur of the moment, while cruising O'ahu's streets and highways, I can run my fingers along its glossy surface, reminding me of the white-crested beauties that await the end of my day.

Lucky you live Hawai'i, as we say. I feel sorry for my landlocked friends who can only surf virtual waves on a computer. Sitting on their *'ōkole* in front of a video screen is hardly the same thing. If just once in their lives they could paddle out and catch a real wave—feel the burn in their arms and the salt spray in their faces. Then they'd know that this ride is nothing like the imaginary ones. Corky McDahl would tell them. If he were still alive.

When I finally pulled in front of HPD's art deco headquarters, the Mercedes, behind me now by about eight car lengths, also pulled to the curb. I sat in my Impala and waited a full minute. The Mercedes didn't move. I waited another minute. So did the Mercedes. As I prepared to wait another five, the big black sedan pulled from the curb and slowly drove by, windows so dark that I couldn't make out the driver or passengers. No doubt about it. I had been followed.

Inside HPD's photo lab I caught up with crack police photographer Creighton Lee, whose expert shots often proved a prosecutor's best friend. Creighton could size up a crime scene in seconds and capture just the right views of the crucial evidence.

"Creighton—howzit?" I grabbed his meaty right hand and we shook by hooking thumbs, local-style.

"Kai, brah," he said in a soft-spoken pidgin totally at odds with his thick fire-hydrant frame. "Surprise' you not up on da Nort' Shore. Big swell, brah. *Beeeg!*"

Creighton was not only a prodigy with the camera, but also a dedicated soul surfer. He usually rode his twelve-foot tanker in knee-high fun stuff, having little ambition for anything bigger, let alone the infamous North Shore titans.

"Not surfing today, brah," I told Creighton in my own pidgin. "Working one case. You like help me, or what?"

"Shoots." The crack photographer shrugged in agreement.

"Remembah dat California surfer wen' wipe out Christmas Eve at Waimea?"

"Da big wipeout? Da guy dat die?"

"Yeah, da same one," I said. "Da widow no can collect on da life insurance. Two hundred gran', brah."

"Ho!" Creighton raised his thick black brows.

"She hire me to prove him dead."

"How you goin' do dat? Da guy been gone since Christmas—da sharks eat 'em, bruddah."

"I figgah dat," I explained, "but I need one photo of his board, plus anyt'ing else you got on da case."

Creighton disappeared for a while, then returned with an accident report and photos of Corky's board, recovered near Sunset Beach the morning after his wipeout. The Californian had ridden a "big gun," also called an "elephant gun." Legendary surfer Buzzy Trent coined the term in the late fifties. Trent reportedly told his shaper, Joe Quigg, "You don't go out hunting elephants with a BB gun, you hunt elephants with an elephant gun. Make me an elephant gun to shoot big waves."

Corky's narrow, stiletto-like gun measured nearly eleven feet with a deep rocker, pin tail, pointed nose, and single fin. Its red and white stripes resembled a candy cane—appropriate for Christmas Eve. Pockmarks in Corky's board showed evidence of being ripped by coral and rock. No sign of shark bites. However, the absence of crescent-shaped *puka* didn't necessarily mean he had escaped the tiger sharks himself.

A Sunset Beach woman reportedly had pulled the fallen surfer's board from the water on Christmas morning and then, for whatever reason, waited nearly twenty-four hours to contact police, who examined and photographed it on the day after Christmas. The surfboard evidently still remained in the possession of this woman, since Corky's next of kin—I guess, Summer—had declined to claim it.

The police report told the story of Corky's wipeout much as his wife and the *Advertiser* had told it. After riding "the wave of his life," he was pounded by three successive twenty-footers and not seen again. A several-day search by Coast Guard, fire department, and HPD teams turned up no trace of the missing surfer, except for the battered candy cane-striped board.

After thanking Creighton for his help I wheeled my Impala back to Maunakea Street while pondering Corky's disappearance. His widely reported wipeout had all the earmarks of a big-wave catastrophe. Each winter, unwary *malihini*—newcomers like Corky McDahl—journey to the islands to challenge Hawai'i's fabled waves. Each winter, tragically, one or more may meet his fate. Knowing firsthand the power and massiveness of Waimea's winter surf, I began to sincerely doubt that Summer's husband had skipped out on her and their baby.

From what I had learned about Corky so far, he probably wasn't my favorite kind of surfer—an aggressive upstart pushing to join the pro circuit, and typically a wave hog who believes he *owns* a wave. If you so much as stroke for the same wave, they go ballistic. A wave hog in the lineup can ruin an entire session.

One day on a beautiful hollow curl at Populars, a guy took off next to me and shot within inches of my board. As a courtesy to a fellow surfer already on the wave, I pulled out.

Astonishingly, after riding this beauty all to himself, the guy paddled straight for me, cursing and threatening that if I so much as came near him on a wave, he was going to "beat the sh— out of me." I paddled away. He had no concept of community, of the brotherhood and sisterhood of wave riders. His selfish vision of the lineup included no one but himself.

Why Corky reminded me of this experience I'm not sure— his arrogant eyes or snarly smile? You can't tell that much from a photo. Or can you?

four

"A high-surf advisory is in effect for all North- and West-facing shores," said the wrought-up voice on the radio as my Chevy purred through pineapple fields and coffee groves on Kamehameha Highway, heading for Haleʻiwa. "On the west side, Mākaha is reporting in at fifteen to eighteen. On the North Shore, Sunset and Pipeline, eighteen to twenty-plus. Waimea is the big story: occasional twenty-five foot sets, or higher . . ." The excited voice paused. "Be careful out there today. Expert surfers only!"

My throat felt suddenly dry. It got even dryer when I crested the ridge overlooking the panorama of the entire North Shore. Across the wide blue horizon, one mammoth wave after another was creaming the turquoise sea. Had I been looking less at the surf and more in my rearview mirror, I might have noticed sooner that black Mercedes behind me again. Even so, it wasn't the Mercedes that was parching my throat. It was the waves.

My cousin Alika had agreed to meet me at a shop called Surf 'n Sea in Haleʻiwa, near the old two-lane bridge by the harbor. Corky's hangout during his last days, Haleʻiwa town featured an eclectic blend of old and new, of local and cosmopolitan, of traditional and trendy. Tin-roofed Matsumoto's General Store, famous for its shave ice, stood shoulder to shoulder with glitzy eateries, new age art galleries, and designer boutiques. Cruising through town I whiffed roasting garlic, sizzling veggie burgers, freshly brewed Kona coffee, grilling *mahi mahi,* and coconut-scented surfboard wax. And I eyed countless boards for sale. Despite the proliferation of upscale surfing-themed retailers that sell more logo apparel than boards, Hale'iwa still boasts more bona fide surf shops per capita than any other town on earth, living up to its nickname—Surf City.

Inside Surf 'n Sea, a rustic country surf shop with a rambling plank porch, I wandered among the racks of gleaming boards by T & C, Robert August, Stewart, Ben Aipa, Donald Takayama, and lots more. Leaning in to get a closer look at a nine-seven carbon fiber Velzy was cousin Alika, his coffee brown eyes as focused and intent as an airline pilot inspecting his ship before takeoff.

"Eh, *haole* boy!" Alika glanced up from the black surfboard and flashed a roguish grin, his deep, resonant voice filling the surf shop like the thrum of a bass fiddle. He extended his muscular brown arm and we shook local-style.

"Howzit, Alika?" I looked up at my cousin, towering over me in board shorts and a bulging tank top emblazoned with "Hawaiian Superman."

From his steel grip and imposing physique, you could tell that Alika Kealoha surfed big waves. His shoulders were wide and his arms massive, and his torso was shaped in a powerful *V.* He was a brawny iron-hard Atlas of a man.

If anybody knew Waimea, it was my Hawaiian cousin. Off the top of his head he could recite the various swells and their directions, the correct lineups for each, the dangerous riptides, and the sometimes risky shore breaks; he could also tell you who rode the biggest wave ever, who took the nastiest wipeout, who got hurt, who disappeared and was lost or found, and who died outright. With only a little prompting Alika remembered Corky McDahl's wipeout.

"Da *haole* surfah dat wipe out on Christmas Eve?" Alika asked me. "Da one dey nevah fin'?"

"Dat's him. You evah see him surf? Candy cane board, blon' hair, *attitude* . . ."

"Maybe at Chun's Reef. If dat him, brah, he OK for one mainland surfah. But bettah he wen' sit on da beach and watch us guyz, yeah? Big Waimea not fo' beginnahs."

"You surfing Waimea when he wipe out? Or your frien's?"

"Not me, brah, but maybe Bolo or Māpuna or Puka," Alika said, referring to his surfing buddies.

"Can ask 'em today?"

"Shoots," the Hawaiian Superman replied.

Out in the gravel lot we climbed into Alika's rusted-out Toyota truck, knobby tires crusted with red dirt. In the bed lay two big guns—sunshine yellow and lime green—similar in size and stiletto shape to Corky's missing board.

As my Hawaiian cousin wound through the gears and the tires began to sing on the blacktop, I recalled today's surf report for Waimea: *occasional twenty-five foot sets, or higher.*

This was a rare occurrence. Only a large winter swell, generated in the North Pacific and headed in just the right direction, causes waves to break like that inside the bay.

On these special days, liquid mountains loom on the horizon, sweep around the point, and explode with the percussion of a volcano. The booms can be heard halfway to Haleʻiwa. The mile-wide bay transforms into a colossal outdoor amphitheater peopled by surfers and photographers and spectators from around the world. The road surrounding the bay chokes with double-parked cars. The lot at the beach park jams. Waimea takes on the elevated mood and bustle of a world-class amusement park. A Disneyland of waves.

But for big-wave riders this is serious business. The potential thrill of a lifetime can become, in unfortunate cases, the *end* of a lifetime. Mark Foo, drowned in 1994 at Mavericks, said it best: "If you want to experience the ultimate thrill, you have to be willing to pay the ultimate price."

When Corky wiped out, there was undoubtedly no shortage of photographers on hand with powerful telephoto lenses that can pick out a tattoo a quarter mile away. But since the wipeout occurred after sundown, the light would not have been best. The news clippings said a few bystanders had watched him get pounded by the first of several twenty-footers. No one reported seeing him after that.

As we approached Waimea, I noticed the bell tower of the Mission of Saints Peter and Paul soaring over the bay, familiar to surfers around the world. Less well known is the ancient cliff-top Mahuka *heiau,* or temple, for human sacrifice just beyond. Both the bell tower and the *heiau* have always suggested to me the sacredness of the bay. For surfers, coming here represents a pilgrimage, a confrontation with the ultimate power, and maybe even a meeting with destiny.

This morning the bell tower cast its long shadow across Waimea's wide beach, where countless caution signs pierced the sand like errant spears: High Surf . . . Hazardous Conditions . . . No Swimming . . . Beach Closed.

Despite these warnings, two surfers were paddling out to join many others in the distant lineup, where one of those liquid mountains was just now steaming in. As it jacked up, a dozen surfers flailed their arms and tried to climb over the massive cresting wave. Some few tempted their fate, turning and plunging down the almost vertical cliff.

Booooom! The mountain detonated in the bay.

"Chance 'um, Kai?" Alika's brown eyes taunted me as he pulled his truck into the jammed lot and parked illegally on a grassy strip.

Dry mouth again.

We stepped out and Alika nudged me. "Grab one board." He pointed to the two guns in the truck's bed.

Booooom! Another mammoth crashed, shaking the ground beneath us. A shiver of fear ran through me.

"Bettah do da interviews first." I wasn't deliberately stalling, but I wasn't in any hurry to paddle into those giants either.

"Da surfahs you need fo' interview stay in da waves, brah," my cousin replied, "not on da beach."

five

If I was going to go tight in the chest, to start breathing fast and feeling weak-kneed, or get butterflies in my stomach—if I was going to panic, the full-blown signs would appear now.

Had the unlucky Corky McDahl shown these telltale signs? I didn't know and right now I didn't care. My only job was to keep them away from me.

"No Fear . . . No Fear . . ." I said a little mantra to focus myself and stay loose.

I stripped off my aloha shirt and khakis, revealing the board shorts I was wearing underneath and the shark bite on my chest that Alika always referred to as my "tattoo."

Alika handed me a chunk of wax and I began reluctantly rubbing it onto the deck of his lime green gun. Out in the distant lineup riders and their surfboards looked like ants clinging to toothpicks. Little more than specks. Each breaker jacked up three or four times higher than the boards cutting white trails down it. The swell was still rising.

"Ho, brah!" Alika pointed toward the roaring bay. "Let's paddle out." I took a deep breath and tried to exhale.

We jogged down the beach to the water. The cool February sea and hiss of the distant foam gave me a few more shivers. The glassy surface near the beach lay deceptively calm, but suddenly an overhead shorebreak wave slammed the beach like a guillotine. We waited for a lull again, then mounted our guns and paddled quickly through the danger zone.

I am not an experienced big wave rider. The few surfers who are form an elite cadre whose door Corky McDahl was knocking on when he got knocked off by those twenty footers. I've often heard the names of big-wave pioneers of the '50s and '60s uttered by young surfers like Corky with reverence—if not a tinge of envy.

Greg Noll earned the nickname "Da Bull" for aggressively charging the biggest waves anybody of his day had ever ridden; Buzzy Trent, the consummate, muscle-packed athlete, resembled a Greek god; Jose Angel, all-around waterman, tragically died diving for black coral; Fred Van Dyke, the "Iron Man" of big wave riding, survived unimaginable wipeouts; Ricky Grigg, surfer and oceanographer, charted some of Hawai'i's famous reef breaks; Eddie "Would Go" Aikau vanished in the Moloka'i Channel while paddling to save a stranded boat crew; and Mākaha legend George Downing, to this day, directs the big wave competition at Waimea in Eddie's name. The roll call of legends also includes familiar names like Brewer, Brown, Cabell, Cole, Curren, Froiseth, Hemmings, Hoffman, Hollinger, Muñoz, Quigg, Strange, and such modern-day heroes as Ken Bradshaw, Laird Hamilton, Brian Keaulana, and the unfortunate Mark Foo. Striving to become one of them, had Corky—like Foo—paid the ultimate price?

Alika and I paddled for what seemed like a half mile deep into the bay. My arms felt tight, no matter how many "No

Fear" mantras I said. In the lull between sets we paddled into the lineup, then over to three surfers on the edge of the pack. One looked like a brown bear. The second, in a red rash guard, was tiny by comparison. The third's scalp was shaved clean—*bolohead*. A bear, a shrimp, and a skinhead.

"Howzit, Bolo?" Alika asked the shaved head. "Howzit, Māpuna, Puka?" He turned to the bear and his tiny friend in red. "Dis my cousin, Kai."

"Howzit, Kai . . . ? Howzit . . .? Howzit?" All three responded in turn, checking me out on Alika's lime green gun.

"Kai one private eye," Alika told his three friends. "One Surfing Detective—Magnum P.I. kine."

"You really one P.I.?" asked the big brown bear whose name, Māpuna, meant "bubbling spring." He was the biggest spring I'd ever seen.

"Yeah, maybe you try help with my case?"

"Us guyz?" The three looked at one another, then broke into laughter.

"Yeah, you guyz." I said. "You know dat California surfah dat wipe out Christmas Eve? His name Corky McDahl."

"Nah," said the small one called Puka, a nickname meaning "hole." "Don' know no Corky."

"Maybe you wen' see him in da lineup—Waimea—day befo' Christmas?"

"What his board look like?" asked Bolo.

"Like one candy cane."

"I seen dat board, brah," little Puka said.

"Here at Waimea?"

"Nah—where wuz it?" Puka thought for a minute. "Ehukai . . . ? Sunset . . . ?"

"You remembah da guy—blon', green eyes . . . ?"

"Nah, but da board—yeah. Sunset, da guy wuz surfing Sunset."

Alika turned to the other two. "You know da guy?"

"Nah," they both said.

"But," bear-like Māpuna adjusted his giant frame on his slim board, "my frien' Ham tol' me he surf Waimea when da *haole* guy ate it."

"Your frien' Ham saw da wipeout?" I asked.

"Dat's what he say. Ham say da *haole* guy bin bury undah da soup, brah. Nevah come up, you know? *Nevah.*"

"Your frien' Ham here today?"

"Nah," Māpuna said.

"Ham working . . . Paradise Sandwich Bar," Puka added, "In Haleʻiwa."

"Tanks, eh?" I said. "Alika, we goin' talk with Ham, sooner da bettah?" I tried not to sound too hopeful.

"You got your detective scoops." Alika flashed a dangerous grin. "Now les' *chance ʻum.*"

I swallowed hard.

The bay lay eerily calm. A big set hadn't rolled through for several minutes. We sat on our boards and waited, which only made me more edgy. I started thinking about Summer. Why did I feel responsible for making things right? Her footloose husband had brought on her misfortune, not me.

"Outside!" Bolo yelled and paddled furiously toward the open sea. Little Puka and mammoth Māpuna followed. Alika and I paddled too. And behind us, the whole pack.

Out on the horizon where the sapphire sky met the sea, an ominous jade mass was building. It was dark and impenetrable, so thick the sun couldn't shine through. And it was rising.

"Outside! someone else yelled.

"Ho!"

"Big, big, *beeeg!*"

The jade mountain was coming. And there would be more behind it.

"Paddle, brah, paddle!" Alika barked at me.

After the nearly half mile stroke from the beach to the lineup, this sudden surge burned my arms. But I kept paddling until I caught up with the first jade cliff, just as it was about to let loose. The face looked to be twenty-five feet, easy. Maybe higher. Up, up, up I clawed, and over the top as it passed. *Phew!*

Craning my neck back, I watched the enormous white lip forming that would soon pound the bay. I was far enough off on the wave's broad shoulder to observe the monster crest and to see Cousin Alika turn, stroke just twice, then drop down the massive face. Alika crouched near the back of his yellow gun and spread his arms wide, like one of those ants I had imagined earlier clinging to a toothpick. His almost vertical drop looked impossible. *Impossible!* The Hawaiian Superman went anyway. I shook my head. No fear.

Boooom! The lip cracked like a thunderbolt. Alika and the jade mountain swept past, leaving only the gauzy lace of blown-back foam.

But there was no time to gaze. The second mountain was coming fast. I felt it rising underneath me. I paddled hard. But not hard enough. I couldn't scratch over the top. Suddenly I found myself gazing down—straight down—a sheer cliff with only one way to go.

I swung my board around into a takeoff position. Thoughts raced through my mind: *feet wide . . . stance low . . . arms spread . . . stay back on the board . . . Holy . . . !*

six

"Kai, brah." Alika paddled back from his ride wearing a million-dollar smile. "Why you let da bes' one go by?"

I shrugged. "I took da nex' one."

Alika glared at me in apparent disbelief.

"It da truth, brah. Da board drop so fas'—*Ho!*—almos' pitch me off."

It *was* the truth. The lime green gun had dropped down that steep face like the bottom fell out, me barely hanging on. In only seconds I had cranked my turn and, just like that, the ride was over.

"*Hana hou!*" my cousin brightened. "Again, brah, again!"

"Nah, let's go to Hale'iwa and find your frien', Ham. Ask 'em 'bout da Christmas Eve wipeout."

Alika frowned.

"I goin' buy lunch," I offered hopefully.

"Laytahs."

Alika stroked out again into those jade cliffs and soon he took another impossible drop. And then another. And another.

It was afternoon before I finally coaxed my Hawaiian cousin out of the water. Luckily when we arrived at Paradise Sandwich Bar in Haleʻiwa, Māpuna's friend Ham was still there.

"Da *haole* guy? He take off too late. Wen' over da falls." Ham spoke to us through the order window as he stacked a deli-style pastrami for Alika, and a *mahi* sandwich for me. Polynesian tattoos covered Ham's dark brown arms, and his chiseled face was crowned by sun-bleached dreadlocks. Alika told me Ham had battled drugs and lost, then wound up at "Oh-Triple-C," the Oʻahu Community Correctional Center in Kalihi, and then in rehab. Struggling to stay clean, he now built sandwiches, surfed, and reported weekly to his parole officer.

"Da red stripe board shot in da air, *way high,*" Ham explained as his fingers danced over the Kaiser roll that was Alika's lunch. "Maybe twenty, t'irty feet—twirling, spinning, brah."

Behind Ham I could see a chrome carousel whirling a half dozen sandwich orders, slips waving like flags in the breeze. Ham watched over my *mahi* sizzling on the grill, then stuck his hand in a plastic container of pickles.

"You like pickles, Alika?" Ham raised his eyes to my cousin.

"Everyt'ing, brah. Da works!"

"So da California surfer's leash snap, or what?" I asked Ham as he flipped my fish fillet and piled pickles and onions and lettuce on Alika's sandwich.

"Fo' sure. Was not hooked to da board anymo'. No way could fly dat high."

"You spot him aftah da wipeout?"

"Nah, *da buggah* gone. Undah da water. Nobody in da lineup see him. Was late, brah, aftah sunset." Ham shrugged his shoulders, tattoos rippling over his brown biceps.

After downing our sandwiches, Alika and I cruised every surf shop in Hale'iwa, trying to track down Corky's missing board and the Sunset Beach woman who had found it. Tropical Rush, Strong Current, Surf n' Sea, again, and all the rest. I questioned everyone I could, but nobody knew much about Corky, other than his well-publicized wipeout. One person did recall seeing the California surfer showboating through Hale'iwa in a BMW convertible. Another mentioned a girlfriend.

"Girlfriend?" I was curious. "Was she blonde and pregnant?" Summer had told me she didn't accompany her husband to Hawai'i, but maybe that wasn't the full story.

"No, this lady had red hair," I was told. "And she didn't look pregnant."

Was Corky pulling the wool over Summer's eyes, stepping out with a redhead in a BMW? Or was it really Corky they had seen?

I left my card at each and every surf shop in Hale'iwa and asked to be called if any board resembling Corky's turned up. Though I had not yet discovered much, Summer was definitely getting her money's worth of my time.

Guiding my Impala back to Honolulu, the allegation that Corky had a redhead girlfriend started bothering me. I decided I wouldn't mention it yet to Summer. In her condition, she needed to think the best of her husband.

It was late afternoon by the time I returned to Maunakea Street. Beyond Mrs. Fujiyama's display cases I caught a glimpse of Leimomi in the back room, stringing a rosebud lei.

Leimomi. We had a date tonight. If I missed it this time, I'd be hard-pressed for an explanation.

Inside my office the red message light was flashing again. I first dialed Leimomi's Punchbowl duplex and I left a message that I would pick her up at seven. My conscience salved, I reached over to my answering machine and pressed Play.

"Hello, Mr. Cooke. This is Summer McDahl. Any chance I could see you? Same place? Tomorrow morning at nine?"

Why not at my office? When I returned Summer's call there was no answer, then a recorded announcement came on—a gravelly male voice with a thick foreign accent said: "Leave message at tone, if you please. Cannot talk right now."

The accent was different than any I had heard before. Middle Eastern? Asian? European? As I left my message I wondered if that voice might belong to the owner of a black Mercedes. I hung up and stared at the phone.

Before leaving my office that afternoon I tried to track down the convertible Corky was allegedly seen driving. There was only a handful of high-line dealerships in Honolulu that traded in pre-owned luxury vehicles like BMWs. I dialed up each number. Aside from trying to sell me one of their fine automobiles, none of the salesmen was much help. I moved on to Honolulu's sole BMW dealership. The salesman who answered was smoother, but just as persistent as the last.

"The Ultimate Driving Machine . . ." he announced, sounding like a TV commercial. "Can I put you behind the wheel?"

"Swell, I'd love to." I gave him hope. "How about tomorrow morning?"

Little did he know I could no more afford a new BMW than a Porsche or Ferrari. I made a mental note to park my old Chevy down the block.

That night I showered and dressed, then drove to Leimomi's duplex. She shared a dingy shack with three other women on the shadowy backside of Punchbowl. A narrow, pot-holed driveway led past two other duplexes to her place, which sat amidst a red tangle of bougainvillea. Aside from this splash of color, her only view was of laundry hanging on the neighboring *lānai*.

A full-time student with a part-time job, Leimomi was constantly strapped. My own threadbare life probably looked bright and glistening by comparison. At least I surfed and, through my work, traveled to the neighbor islands and sometimes to the mainland. Maybe that was part of my attractiveness to her?

Swinging into her dusky lane, I felt the same surge of excitement that I always did approaching her place. And an equally strong twinge of guilt. While the dank duplex gave off a certain moldy, rotting odor, it also smelled like . . . *love*.

This was the place Leimomi and I had discovered each other for the first time, her rusty bedsprings singing a high-pitched siren song that drowned out even her scratchy clock radio. The room got as steamy as a sauna. We stayed in bed through that first night and the whole next day—snoozing, whispering, making love. Leimomi cried. I comforted her. We made love again. Neither of us wanted to leave. By four in the afternoon we got so hungry we ordered two Domino's pizzas and ate them both.

With Leimomi's euphoric first taste of love came, for me, an unspoken responsibility. After our breathless twenty-four hours together in bed, she glommed onto me like a faithful pet. Every time I turned around, she was there. I hadn't counted on that. Sometimes, I had to admit, I longed for a way to slip away without hurting her.

Leimomi was unusually quiet on the ride to dinner at Cafe Diamond Head. She had chosen the Pacific-Rim establishment with its reputation for flamboyant fusion cuisine. Filet mignon *wasabe* with mango-macadamia chutney staked on Kahuku sweet potatoes. That sort of thing. Its high prices did something toward assuaging my guilt.

We sat at a table overlooking the soaring brow of the islands' most famous crater, barely visible in the fading twilight. I glanced at the pricy wine list and ordered a beer. Leimomi did too. We raised our glasses and I toasted Leimomi's beauty and good health. We were off to a good start. Her earlier upset seemed to be wearing off.

Sipping my beer, I noticed two men in black suits sitting across from us who appeared, from their overly formal attire, to be *malihini*. They were an odd pair in this chic Honolulu restaurant, where casual aloha attire was the norm. They kept gazing toward Leimomi, which kind of flattered me. They'd probably never seen a more beautiful island girl.

Just then I made the mistake of mentioning I had surfed that morning at Waimea Bay. The usually soft-spoken Leimomi reacted in a way that set my teeth on edge.

"I wish you wouldn't ride those huge waves," she said stridently. "Surfers get killed, you know."

"I know." I tried to put her mind at ease. "I'm working on a case involving that California surfer who died last Christmas Eve at Waimea. That's why I was there."

"What's to investigate?" she asked, still with a sharpness in her voice that surprised me.

"His insurance company won't pay because of some questions about his wipeout. Like, did he really die? Or was he faking it?"

"What did you find out?"

"Nothing for sure yet. But if he was trying to escape his pregnant wife and the responsibilities of fatherhood, I can think of a lot easier ways."

Leimomi gazed at me silently. Her cheeks colored. "Kai . . ." she began and then stopped.

"What, Lei?" She was starting to worry me.

"I'm thinking . . ." She paused again and tears welled in her eyes. "No, I can't burden you . . . until I'm sure . . ."

"Leimomi, you already have." I was getting agitated. She was dangling a carrot in front of me, though I wasn't sure I wanted to bite it.

"That surfer," she started again, "trying to escape the responsibilities of fatherhood . . ."

"What? Does he remind you of your father? How he skipped out on you and your mother?" I was grasping at something, anything, to steer the conversation away from me, and remembered that Leimomi's dad had been put away for dealing drugs.

"Well, I do wonder about Daddy and I miss him, but that's not what I was thinking about."

"What were you thinking?" I was starting to sweat.

"Kai, I'm pregnant." She studied my face for a response.

"Are you sure?" I asked, my expression frozen.

"I'm over a week late . . ." Leimomi blushed. "I'm always, I mean, I'm usually on time, like a clock."

"OK." My aloha shirt suddenly felt swampy. "Let's not overreact . . . I mean . . . it's perfectly natural. We'll figure something out. Let's stay calm."

"I'd love to have our baby, Kai," she went on, her tears flowing now, "but this isn't . . . the best time in my life . . . not until I finish my courses."

"Are you sure it isn't a false alarm, Lei?" Maybe she had calculated wrong. She sometimes did that, confusing dates or dollar amounts. God, I hoped she was wrong.

"I doubt it. I'm too long overdue."

I sat back in my chair and took another drink of beer, which now tasted pretty flat. I guess it was too late to slip away.

seven

I sat staring into my coffee at Denny's in Waikīkī the next morning. As much as I cared for Leimomi, I knew I didn't want to be the father of her child. *How did I let it go this far?* I tried to picture Leimomi in the same state as Summer, swollen with child, then shook the image out of my head.

Nine o'clock came and went. Summer still hadn't shown.

I tried to focus on the case. What about that gravelly thick accent at the Kāhala phone number Summer had given me? The voice didn't fit her profile. If she or Corky had friends in Hawai'i, they would more likely be people like themselves— transplanted Californians or *kama'āina haole* types, or maybe surfers who sounded local. But not wealthy foreigners who lived in O'ahu's poshest oceanside enclave.

Through the steam swirling skyward from my cup I watched the morning flow of beach-goers and surfers filing down Kapahulu Avenue. No rain today. The sun glowed over Diamond Head and glinted on the tiny shore break of Waikīkī Beach. I gazed down in front of Starbucks, figuring Summer would be hard to miss in the crowd. No sign of her.

At quarter after nine a bakery van painted with a big red heart with the word "Love's" inside it pulled to the curb by the ABC Store next to Starbucks. The driver began unloading donuts and sweet rolls and cinnamon buns destined for Denny's. I sipped my coffee. Then a black Mercedes pulled alongside the van. The van obstructed my view, so I couldn't see who got out. Two doors slammed, then the Mercedes pulled away. I kept my eyes on the van until I heard, behind me, Summer's whispering voice.

"Mr. Cooke?" She edged into the booth across from me. Today's maternity dress was baby blue. "Have you found any evidence yet?" She cut straight to the chase.

"I'm working on it," I said and sipped my coffee. "Yesterday I interviewed some surfers who saw Corky at different North Shore breaks. One named Ham Makanani was in the water Christmas Eve at Waimea and saw the whole thing. He doesn't doubt your husband drowned, but it's going to be tough to locate any tangible evidence."

"But isn't tangible evidence what we need to convince Mr. Gold?"

"More or less, and I will pursue every lead . . ." I thought for a moment about her husband's alleged redhead girlfriend.

"I hope you find something"—Summer glanced down at her enormous belly— "before the baby comes."

I followed her gaze and couldn't help but wonder aloud, "Should you have flown here, Summer, with your baby due so soon?"

"I had to make this trip." She peered at me with those intense violet eyes. "Without that insurance money the baby and I are lost."

"What about your family, or Corky's family? Can't they help?"

"Not really." Summer sighed. "Corky was estranged from his parents. He deeply loved his mother, but never got along with his stepfather. A few years ago they moved to Idaho. I don't even know where in Idaho. But Corky's folks never cared much for me. They didn't call or write when Corky died. I thought I'd at least hear from his mother."

"What about your family?"

"Just my mother is left. She lives on social security, from check to check. She usually needs help from me—not the reverse . . ." Summer paused. "If I didn't need that insurance money I wouldn't have come all this way."

The waitress refilled my coffee. I decided to take a different track. "The BMW convertible you mentioned. I'm going to visit the dealership later this morning, but I need more to go on. The model, the color, the year, the license—any specifics would help."

"Well, I'm not a car person." She uttered the phrase distastefully. "Cars, for me, are just a way to get from here to there. But Corky loved expensive, exotic cars, though he could never afford to own the ones he worked on."

"Were there any BMWs, even in California, that he may have detailed?"

"Mmmm . . . there was this one beautiful maroon car with cream-colored leather."

"Was it a convertible?"

"I think so . . ." She paused again. "Yes, the top was cream or beige, the same color as its seats."

"So the only BMW you can remember him working on was a maroon and cream convertible? Any idea what year it was?"

"Brand new. Or almost new."

"Do you remember the owner?"

"Only that it was a California customer." Summer looked puzzled. "But I doubt that car would be here in Hawai'i."

"You're probably right. But it's all we have to go on. I'll check it out with the dealer."

"Will you call me as soon as you find out anything?"

"Of course . . ." I hesitated. "You know, when I called you before, I wasn't sure I dialed the right number. There was a man's voice on the answering machine—an older man with a thick accent."

"I got your message." Summer looked away. She rose, her bulging figure setting her slightly off-balance. "Do you need any more money?"

"No." Evidently she wasn't going to explain the accented voice. "You've given me plenty of money for now."

Summer made her way toward Denny's exit, then down the stairs to street level. Where the Love's bakery van had been, Summer now waited by the curb. A man in a dark suit was talking on a cell phone next to her. Then I noticed he wasn't just standing next to her; he had his free arm hooked into one of hers, as if escorting her.

The black Mercedes pulled up again and Summer and the man climbed into the backseat. It whisked them off in the direction of Diamond Head, leaving me more than curious about Summer's mysterious friends.

Down by the Waikīkī Aquarium, where I had parked under a shady stand of ironwoods, I climbed into my Impala and headed for the BMW dealership. Chances were, if the car Corky was seen in had been purchased or serviced here, the dealer would know about it.

After a few minutes traveling 'Ewa on Kapi'olani Boulevard, I pulled to the curb just beyond Ward Avenue, parking my old

Chevy out of view from the showroom. I strolled down the street and then through the showroom doors, trying to look as confident as any potential new luxury car buyer.

The mirror-like marble floor reflected an impressive array of German automobiles. While waiting for the salesman I had time to admire them: sedans in midnight blue and metallic silver, a pastel yellow convertible, a flame red sports car. I eyed supple leather seats in one sleek driving machine after another. Had I forty or sixty or eighty grand to drop on a car, this would be a nice place to start.

I had paid only one grand for my thirty-year-old Impala and the grieving widow who sold it to me was very pleased to get that. The car would have gone for less, but somebody had told her it was a classic. A single alloy wheel on the gleaming sport sedan now in my gaze probably cost as much as my entire car. Does that mean the BMW would be more fun? I don't know. But as long as I can ride waves, any wheels that get me and my board to the beach will do fine.

"Can I put you behind the wheel of that sensational M5?" The grinning salesman approached me with his right arm extended. "You must be Mr. Cooke?"

"Yes," I said, shaking his hand, "But one problem—to buy it I'd have to sell my soul."

"Well"—the salesman's smile broadened—"how much is your soul worth?"

"Actually," I said, starting my spiel, "I'm trying to trace a certain BMW. I'm a private investigator."

His smile faded. "Oh, well . . . if I can help."

I handed him my card.

When he glanced at the longboard rider, he perked up again. "Do you know anything about the car?"

"Not much. The deceased's wife can remember only one BMW her husband detailed in his business in California."

"California?" The salesman looked dubious.

"I know. It's a long shot."

"Well, we do buy and sell a lot of cars—and some have out-of-state plates, occasionally."

"The car she remembers was a new or nearly new convertible—maroon with cream-colored leather and top."

The salesman seemed to be scanning his memory. "A few months ago we took in a maroon convertible, but with a black top and no California plates."

"It's worth following up."

"I didn't do the transaction. Another salesman did who's since moved on. Hold on a minute and I'll see what I can find out." He walked from the showroom and disappeared into an inner office.

Minutes later he returned with a handful of stapled forms. "Let's see, we took in the maroon convertible in December . . . December thirteenth . . . and I was wrong about the top. It *was* tan, not black." He studied some figures. "Boy, we got a deal on this." He flipped between pages. "It looks like the seller took way below wholesale bluebook for the vehicle—less than he had to if he would have done his homework. And I remember the car was in great shape."

"What was the owner's name?"

"DiCarlo." The salesman glanced at the colored forms. "Damon DiCarlo of Balboa, California."

"Damn."

"Not the guy you're looking for?"

"Afraid not."

"The car was registered in California," the salesman continued. "And had California plates."

Just then a woman in a silk dress and spiked heels—someone who looked like she could afford a new BMW—strolled in.

"Excuse me a moment." The salesman turned away from me and eagerly approached his new prospect. They talked briefly and then the woman must have uttered something to the effect of "just looking," and the salesman backed off.

"So what happened to this maroon convertible?" I asked as he walked toward me.

"We sold it to an attorney on Bishop Street. But since he's a current customer, technically, I can't give you his name." The salesman held a pink form carelessly within my view, his thumb next to the words "William J. Grossvendt."

"I understand," I said. "Confidentiality and all that."

The salesman winked. Then he seemed to have a flash of inspiration. "Now I remember—not one hour after the new buyer signed for the car, a foreign gentleman came in and wanted it—wanted it badly. He offered to pay more, to fork over a new retail price if I would sell it to him. But I couldn't, of course, because the car was already sold."

"Why do you think he wanted it so much?"

"Well, the strange thing was, we had another maroon convertible—a brand new one—out at the dock ready for pick up. That one must have had the black top I was remembering. Anyway, if the buyer could have waited one day—just one day—it would have been his."

"Did he wait?"

"No, we never saw the man again." The salesman arched his brows.

I thanked him and found my way out. By then he was trying his charm again on the woman in heels.

Down the street, parked alongside the curb, my old Impala looked ancient compared to those shiny BMWs. *It's a classic,* I told myself. *A timeless piece of Americana.* Besides, my longboard fits right in.

eight

I hurried back to Maunakea Street and cracked my Oʻahu phone directory. William J. Grossvendt was listed—both a home phone with an ocean-side Portlock address in Hawaiʻi Kai, and an office number on Bishop Street: Grossvendt, Weller, and Chang, Attorneys at Law. Bishop Street is where the swankiest attorneys in Honolulu hang their shingles, in the high-altitude offices of mirrored skyscrapers. Grossvendt certainly earned enough as a lawyer to purchase a new BMW, so why did he cheap out and buy a used one?

Since it was a Wednesday morning I tried his office first. The phone rang twice and then an upbeat receptionist said, "Good Morning! Grossvendt, Weller, and Chang—specializing in trusts and wills."

"I'd like to speak with Mr. Grossvendt, please."

"One moment, sir." The receptionist connected me, not to Mr. Grossvendt himself, but to a woman I assumed was his assistant or paralegal. She told me that the attorney was unavailable, but asked if I would like to leave a message. When I said I was a PI inquiring about Mr. Grossvendt's BMW convertible, the woman abruptly stopped me in mid-sentence. "Hold, please."

Within seconds attorney William J. Grossvendt himself came on the line.

"Mr. Cooke," said a high, quavering voice, "you have information about my car?"

"Actually, I was going to ask you for some information."

"Have you found it?" the attorney asked excitedly. "Have you found it?" He sounded like a boy who had lost his favorite toy.

"Found what?"

"My BMW convertible!" he said impatiently.

"Is it missing?" I asked naively, hoping for more information.

"Why, it was stolen from my parking garage in early January, not two days after I bought it. It's been missing nearly a month. My assistant said you are a P.I.?" He sounded hopeful.

"Yes. Does HPD have any leads?"

"None," the attorney said. "And it was a professional job. That car had all the high tech anti-theft devices money can buy."

"Sounds like this theft was more about that particular car than about you."

"I wouldn't be so sure." His voice cracked. "I've had cars vandalized before—*keyed,* you know—and have received my share of threats, even death threats. Sometimes heirs cut from Grandma's will blame me, the attorney. They think I've taken their money. When my BMW was stolen, I had in mind a few people who might be responsible."

"I suppose there's a chance of that."

"So what's in this for you, Mr. Cooke?" the attorney asked in his anxious voice.

"I'm pursuing an entirely different case, but I think your car may somehow be related to it. The death of a California surfer at Waimea Bay last Christmas Eve."

"I heard about that. He died on a huge wave, right?"

"Right. And he was driving a BMW around on the North Shore before his wipeout. The car has been missing since his death—maybe the same car you bought."

"I really loved that car. And I'd love to have it back."

"Why don't you take the insurance money and buy another? I bet the dealership could get one just like it."

"I'm sentimental about that very car. My girlfriend helped me pick it out." He hit a somber note. "And she's since left the islands."

"I'll let you know what I turn up."

"Much appreciated."

"By the way," I said, "do you know my attorney friend, Tommy Woo?"

"Tommy? Yeah, I know him. But he's a sore subject around here."

"Why?" I asked.

The attorney cleared his throat. "One evening my former wife and I were at a party at Oʻahu Country Club—a very elegant white-tie affair—and Tommy was playing piano. On his break Tommy comes over to where we're sipping Dom Pérignon with a CEO friend, of a Big Five company, you know, and Tommy says, "Hey, Bill, did you hear the one about the Siamese twins hookers who offered a 'double-your-pleasure' guarantee . . . ?"

"Siamese twins hookers?" I recalled one of Tommy's crudest jokes.

"Yeah, the punch line made the CEO turn blue, I tell you. And my former wife, well, she looked as if she'd been bitten by a snake. That Tommy Woo, he's a prize all right."

I had to laugh. "I'll let you know if I find your car."

When the trust attorney hung up I wondered what Tommy Woo would say about stuffy Grossvendt, his blue-blood ex-wife, and the Big Five CEO. I pictured Tommy adjusting his tortoiseshell glasses with a flourish, puffing cherry blend in his meerschaum pipe, and uttering profoundly: "If they can't take a joke, f– 'em."

This mysterious car business wasn't making much sense. The convertible was registered in California, turned up in Hawai'i, and was purchased below wholesale by a Honolulu dealership, then sold to a Bishop Street attorney, *then* stolen from him two days later. Could it be linked to Corky McDahl?

I phoned information for Balboa, California, and got the number for Damon DiCarlo, the registered owner. DiCarlo's address was on East Ocean Front. From what I remembered about real estate in this pricy area of Orange County, Ocean Front was an exclusive seaside lane on the Newport peninsula. It adjoined the Balboa Channel and the famous body board spot called "The Wedge," a powerful, treacherous shore break that can hammer the unwary. Wicked huge swells pump up against a rock jetty, then slam the steep beach, spraying sand and foam every which way. It is one easy spot to break your neck.

I placed the call to DiCarlo. After four rings a melodic, Brando-like voice said: "Damon here. You know the routine. Leave a message and I'll call . . ."

I left my name and number, mentioning the BMW he sold. I wondered if this Damon would bother to phone back a complete stranger in Hawai'i.

I returned to the phone book and called all the surf shops Alika and I had visited in Hale'iwa. Still no sign of Corky's board. The candy cane had seemingly vanished. I wondered if the Sunset Beach woman who first found the board had kept it, and if so, why? By all accounts, it had been badly damaged. Were she and Corky's alleged red-haired girlfriend one and the same? I wasn't even sure if this elusive redhead existed.

Gradually I began to picture Summer's marriage to the California surfer as less than ideal. The young couple certainly remained apart for long stretches. But could they really be scamming the insurance company? I had a deep sense that Summer was not type to do such a thing. She was nervous, yes, and anxious. And she was evasive about certain details. Yet an underlying naive sincerity in her character seemed at odds with the idea of fraud. But I had to factor in the dark-suited men who "escorted" her in that hearse of a Mercedes. And that brought up questions. They weren't simple questions like "Did Corky really die?" or "Did Corky skip out on his wife and new baby?" These were more complex questions buried beneath the one she and the insurance agent were asking. Trouble was, I wasn't sure what they were.

It was time to fit in a quick session in Waikīkī. I hopped into my Impala and headed for Classic Surfboards on Kapahulu Avenue to get some wax.

Classic Surfboards is a groovy, sixties-style surf shop lined with more used boards than new, and hardly any glitzy logo apparel. The shop's motto warms my heart: "No Gimmicks, No Bullshit, Just Surfing." A short walk from Waikīkī Beach, Classic Surfboards attracts local surfers and tourists alike. Since it can be cheaper to buy a board there than to rent one day after day at the beach, some boards for sale are dinged old tankers;

but you can also find some nice ones at good prices. Surf'n Jenny, the sandy-haired proprietor and mother of two, always tells sellers: "Ask the very lowest price you will accept and your board will sell fast." I sold a ten foot T & C here in one day.

Inside the shoebox-sized shop I made a beeline for the glass counter piled high with cylinders of pastel-colored surfboard wax. My favorite is coconut-scented "Sex Wax." Expressly for warm water, this milky-white wax has an ambrosial island fragrance that never fails to raise the hairs on the back of my neck. I selected one disk of wax the size of a hockey puck and set it on the counter.

"Hi, Kai!" Jenny greeted me with a big grin. "Heading up to the North Shore?"

"Nah, I was just there yesterday at Waimea. Nearly killed myself on a thirty-footer." I exaggerated. "Today I'm heading out to Pops."

"Kai, for Waimea you need a gun." She looked concerned. "That nine-six nose rider of yours isn't built for big waves."

"I know, I borrowed a gun from my cousin Alika. It was OK. Didn't suit me exactly, but close enough."

"I took in a big gun nearly a month ago. It's got an amateur patch job, but it would have sold instantly if she hadn't put such a high price on it," Jenny explained. "She wants $350."

"A woman is selling a big gun? Not many women surf Waimea."

"She said she's selling it for a friend who left the island," Jenny replied. "I'm surprised she didn't put it in a shop in Hale'iwa, 'cuz the address she gave is on the North Shore. The board, though, was made in California."

"Wait a minute. Can I see this board?"

"It's over there between those two tankers." Jenny pointed to a wall lined with boards standing in file on their tails. There it was—red and white stripes like a candy cane, its narrow pointed nose rising nearly a foot above the longboards next to it.

Jenny gingerly plucked it out like a stick of gum from a pack. California surfboard label. No leash. And those telltale stripes.

"I want to buy this board." I tried to mask my rush of emotion. "How much does she want for it again?"

Jenny drew a card from a small file box behind the counter and glanced at it. "Too much, Kai. You're a good customer. How about I cut my commission and drop the price to three hundred."

"Did it come in with a leash?"

"You don't want that leash. It was sliced right in two—I only got the part still hooked to the board."

"Sliced or snapped? I think a surfer wiped out on this board at Waimea—the leash could have snapped or been shredded by coral."

"No, this one looks sliced like bologna."

"Do you still have it?"

"I threw it in the scrap bin in back. But that was weeks ago—and I'm not the only one who goes back there."

"I'll pay cash if you can find me that leash and give me the woman's name and address."

"Sorry, Kai, I can't give out her personal information. I promise all my customers confidentiality."

"I understand," I replied. Knowing Jenny's integrity, I didn't want to offend her or push my luck. To avoid trading in stolen boards, she was a stickler for gathering and protecting detailed information on her clients.

She set the card on the counter and covered it with the wax I had put there. Then she stepped into the back room.

I glanced at the card. The seller's address and other vital information were concealed under the wax. Out of respect for Jenny, I wasn't about to move it. On the edges of the card not covered by the wax, I could just make out a first name, "Maya," and the last four digits of a phone number. That was enough. I knew already the North Shore prefix. So I had myself a complete number. *Bingo!*

Jenny returned with a four-foot section of leash. I carefully studied the severed end. When a surfboard leash snaps in the heat of a wipeout, the broken surface looks irregular and jagged—with tiny peaks and valleys and burrs. But this leash appeared to have been sliced clean, as if with a knife. A few fine, curved parallel lines over the otherwise flat surface suggested the sawing movement of a sharp blade.

"Thanks for the cord," I said. "It may come in handy."

"A broken leash? Handy?"

I peeled off three of Summer's rumpled Ben Franklins.

Jenny eyed the bills. "I love cash."

"That makes two of us."

With sliced leash and badly-patched candy cane in hand, I stepped from the surf shop beaming.

nine

Nearly eleven feet of surfboard proved too much even for my spacious Chevy. Luckily, I always carry along a pair of soft roof racks. Within minutes I had positioned the racks on the wide teal roof, tightened the nylon straps inside the cabin, and lashed the candy-striped red board securely in place.

Back on Maunakea Street I maneuvered the lengthy gun between the cashier's counter and refrigerated display cases at Fujiyama's, and up the orange shag stairs. I got a few looks from Mrs. Fujiyama and her *lei* girls. Leimomi actually frowned. Did she think this telltale board proved her boyfriend had taken up big wave riding? Considering Leimomi's condition, that probably made me as irresponsible to her as Corky McDahl had been. The parallel made me wince.

Inside my office I set Corky's board on a rail along my longest wall and checked out the repair job. Amateur, as Surf'n Jenny had said. The patched board looked dappled like a roan pony, its dings unpainted, wavy, and irregular. I couldn't believe the seller had put such a high price on a wreck like this.

Before examining it further, I noticed the familiar blinking light of my answering machine and checked my messages.

"Mr. Cooke," said a singsong female voice, "this is Mr. DiCarlo's secretary returning your call from his office in Costa Mesa, California. Mr. DiCarlo is out of town, but he would appreciate any information you could provide him about his stolen car . . ."

Mr. DiCarlo's stolen car? Was this a twice-stolen car—heisted from both DiCarlo and Grossvendt? And if the former hadn't turned it in to the BMW dealership, who had?

Quickly I returned the secretary's call.

"DiCarlo Inc.," answered the same voice that had left the message.

I told her who I was and she became helpful.

"You've found Mr. DiCarlo's car?"

"Not exactly. I've found that it has been stolen—again. Not from Mr. DiCarlo, but from the car's new owner here in Hawai'i."

"In Hawai'i?" The singsong voice hit a high note.

"That's right. Did Mr. DiCarlo ship his car to Honolulu?"

"Not that I know of."

"Where is he now?"

"Well, this is a bit of a coincidence—Mr. DiCarlo is vacationing in Hawai'i."

"That *is* a coincidence. Are you in touch with him?"

"I can be."

"Would you give me his number or ask him to call me?"

"I'll ask him to call you."

"Fine," I said, feeling like we were finally getting somewhere. "One last question. Does the name Corky McDahl sound at all familiar?"

"Corky?" She paused. "Isn't he the fellow who washes Mr. DiCarlo's car?"

Bingo. "He apparently had an auto detailing business in Newport Beach."

"Then that's him, yes. Corky cleaned Mr. DiCarlo's car."

"The BMW convertible—maroon with cream leather?"

"Yes."

"Could Corky have taken that convertible to Hawai'i?"

"Why would he do that? Why would Mr. DiCarlo allow him to?"

"I don't know. It doesn't make sense. Are you sure you can't give me Mr. DiCarlo's phone number in Hawai'i?"

"I'd like to, Mr. Cooke. You sound very honest and sincere, but I can't. I'm sorry. I will call him with your number right away."

"What kind of business is he in?"

"Import-export."

"What sort of products?"

"The products change depending on what's available."

"Did his business take him to Hawai'i?"

"Mr. DiCarlo travels extensively on business," she said, "mostly to Mexico and South America. He speaks fluent Spanish."

"That so? I'd really appreciate hearing from Mr. DiCarlo."

"You will, I'm sure."

I then phoned the number Summer had given me and got that heavy accent again. "Leave message at tone, if you please . . ."

I asked Summer to call me, mentioning vaguely that I had made some progress.

Next I placed a call to the North Shore number of "Maya." A young woman answered.

"Maya?" I asked.

"No," she corrected me. "Maya doesn't live here anymore."

"Where's here?"

"Who's calling, please?" She sounded agitated.

"Kai. I was a surfing buddy of Corky McDahl."

"You have the wrong number."

"Where might I find Maya now?"

Click.

No worries. I pulled out my handy directory that lists the addresses of all people on Oʻahu by phone number, turned to the prefix "638," then scanned down until I found the last four digits of the number I'd just called. It belonged to an address off Kamehameha Highway called Kē Nui Road that fronts the ocean.

Kē Nui is a road of big wave riders. It looks out on the famous breaks of the North Shore—Sunset, Pipeline, and nearby Pūpūkea. Down the road a hop, skip, and jump is Waimea Bay. Kē Nui is near the center, in other words, of the surfing universe. Legends have called this street home—along with some young hopefuls. It didn't surprise me that Corky, by way of this woman named Maya, was associated with Kē Nui Road.

In less than an hour, with Corky's board lashed on top, my Impala rolled into the sandy lot overlooking blown-out Sunset Beach. The wind-whipped sea was the color of marbled jade— dark green riddled with stark white. Signs posted on the beach warned: High Surf . . . Dangerous Currents . . . No Swimming . . . Beach Closed. Above these signs, Day-Glo orange flags stood stiff in the wind.

Nobody—swimmer, boogie boarder, or surfer—was out today. Not just because of the signs, but because even the regular crew at Sunset knows when to battle and when to retreat. The roar of the tumultuous waves resembled the H-1 Freeway at rush hour—amplified tenfold. It was a din that filled the air completely.

From Sunset Beach, I drove a short quarter mile to oceanfront Kē Nui Road, where the surf continued to roar. Maya's address was attached to a cottage with shake roof whose beach side stood on stilts in the sand at the high tide mark. You couldn't get much closer to the water than this without swimming.

I knocked and soon a wet-haired surfer girl stood before me in a string bikini top and skin-tight jeans. Her baby-white skin and pale blue eyes had mainland written all over them. She appeared to be about Leimomi's age.

"Is Maya here?" I whiffed the fresh scent of lavender on her.

"No," she said in a voice lower pitched than the young woman I had spoken with on the phone, but no less defiant.

"I'm a friend of Corky McDahl. I wondered if Maya could tell me anything about his wipeout—just to soothe my mind. I still have his photo." I showed her the snapshot Summer had given me.

The surfer girl didn't respond.

"Does Maya still live here?" I tried again.

"No."

"Do you know where I can reach her?"

"No."

"Did she leave a forwarding address? Or a phone number?"

"No."

"Was Corky Maya's boyfriend?"

"You'd have to ask one of my roommates."

"May I?"

"They're not here," she said matter-of-factly.

"Would you please have them call me at this number?" I handed her my card, hoping the surfer image on it would reinforce my pose as Corky's wave-riding buddy.

"I can't guarantee they will." She shoved the card deep into a pocket of her jeans.

If she wasn't hiding something, someone was. Why else would she be so rude?

I knew the North Shore wasn't all good vibes and big waves. There were drug-related crimes and violence, like everywhere else. Recently at a birthday party at Laniākea two men were stabbed to death and several others beaten senseless. The culprits slipped away into a dark underworld the tourist bureau doesn't advertise. That makes the North Shore not a place to go poking around into other people's business, especially the wrong people. You might end up dead.

Up the road from Sunset Beach I stopped in at the Foodland, a chain supermarket and larger than you'd expect in the country setting of Pūpūkea. I wandered around until I found the crack seed display. I pulled a small package from the hanging rack and headed for the checkout line. A local guy, who from the width of his shoulders looked like he surfed, rang me up. I pulled out my wallet containing the photo of Corky. Handing a couple bills to the clerk, I flashed the picture.

"Evah see dis guy?"

"Dat's da guy wen' wipe out at Waimea . . ."

"Corky, yeah. Evah see his girlfriend? Redhead."

"Maya? Ho, nice!" He smiled suggestively.

"Yeah, Maya. Know where I can find her?"

"She live on da beach at Sunset . . ."

"Yeah, but her roommate say she gone."

"Gone?"

"Any idea where?"

"Maybe upcountry Maui?" the clerk said. "I t'ink she from Makawao."

"You sure?"

"Dunno fo' sure, brah." He shrugged.

"T'anks, eh?"

He was still leering at the thought of Maya as he handed me my bag.

ten

The bell tower at the Mission of Saints Peter and Paul loomed ominously over Waimea Bay as I glided by, heading for Haleʻiwa town.

About halfway there, a black Mercedes with dark windows flashed by in the opposite direction. I couldn't have sworn it was Summer's escorts, but the men in the front seat looked hauntingly familiar. Were they going where I had been? Kē Nui Road? Pūpūkea Foodland?

At Surf ʻn Sea in Haleʻiwa I searched for a shaper from Oregon named Skipper who surfed occasionally with Cousin Alika. Although not born in Hawaiʻi, Skipper knew North Shore breaks and boards as well as many local surfers.

Surfboards in various degrees of ding patching leaned against the walls of the shop. The air was thick with the chemical odor of uncured resin. The floor felt sticky under my feet and was plastered with castoff strips of cotton-soft and resin-hardened fiberglass cloth. Skipper wore a surgical mask beneath his grey eyes and close-clipped hair of peroxide orange. A diamond stud in his left ear lobe glittered.

While I watched, Skipper squeegeed resin onto the deck and one rail of a surfboard—a gun with a slot-like hole in the deck where another surfer's fin had apparently dug in. In other words, the board had been "skegged."

When he was finished I showed Skipper Corky's poorly patched board and severed leash.

"Any idea who might have repaired this candy cane?"

"Ugly." Skipper shook his head. "No shop in Hale'iwa did this. I'd bet it was patched in somebody's garage. Maybe that guy out in Mokule'ia? I've never met him. He's military—from Schofield Barracks." Skipper eyed the board. "How much did you give for it?"

"Three hundred."

Skipper rolled his eyes.

"I needed the board for a case I'm working on," I explained, "the death of that California surfer who wiped out at Waimea on Christmas Eve."

"I remember that guy," said the shaper. "Too bad."

"You knew him?"

"Not really. Just to say hello. He brought in his lady once." Skipper raised his dusty brows. *"Nice."*

"What was her name?"

"I don't know, but I heard they were getting married and all. Then he wipes out at Waimea." He shrugged. "Foxy lady too—leggy, long red locks. She was older, but nice."

"Older? How much older?"

"Older than him. In her thirties, maybe."

"Any idea where I can find her?"

"Sunset Beach, I think."

"She's not there anymore," I said.

"Then I don't have a clue." Skipper shook his head.

As I left Hale'iwa town I turned west toward Mokule'ia, beyond which the paved road ends and the Waianae range drops down to a remote stretch of craggy coastline. Luckily, I didn't have to go that far. On oceanfront Crozier Drive in Mokule'ia, I searched for a novice *ding-meister* working out of his garage.

On the *mauka* side of the street in a carport, a crew-cut *haole* kid in a surgical mask was sanding a surfboard. He looked barely eighteen, skinny, and red-faced above the mask from too much tropic sun on fair skin. I pulled in front of the carport and removed Corky's board from my roof racks.

"You patch surfboards?"

He put down his sandpaper and flipped off the mask. A ring of white resin dust circled his mouth and nose like the outline of a goatee. "You bet. You need a ding repaired?"

I flipped over Corky's gun to display its mottled bottom. "This board has already been patched. I'd just like to know who repaired it."

"It's not the best repair job." He observed its wavy contours. "Hold on . . ." The novice *ding-meister* rubbed the freckles on his nose. "I remember that board."

"You patched it like this?"

"She was in a big hurry," he explained defensively. "She didn't want it done fancy. She wanted it done *fast*. She said she would pay extra if I could finish in two days, instead of my usual week."

"Who was she?"

"A good-look'n babe." He flashed a salacious smile.

"Did you ask her what happened to the board?"

"Didn't need to. She told me she hit a reef at Rocky Point."

"That so?" I replied straight-faced, trying not to betray my disbelief. Rocky Point is a popular winter break between

Sunset and Pipeline. Everybody and his dog is out there on a good day. The reefs at Rocky Point could certainly damage a board, but not this one.

"Hey," said the teenager, "where did *you* get the board?"

"I bought it in town at a surf shop on Kapahulu."

"Oh." He rubbed the resin dust around his chin. "I figured she was going to sell it before she went to Maui."

"Maui?" I said, recalling that the Foodland clerk had said the same. "Did she say where on Maui?"

"Nah." He wrinkled his freckled nose. "Does it matter? Why are you asking all these questions?"

"Just curious."

"Ooohh," he uttered, as if we shared some kind of secret. "Yeah, she makes me curious too."

Back in my office, there was a message waiting for me.

"Kai, I'm worried." It was Leimomi, with that edge in her voice. "I'm really late now. And I feel funny—kind of sick to my stomach. Maybe I'm just worried sick, but I don't feel like eating. And when I do eat, nothing tastes right. All I can keep down are saltine crackers—the only food mother could stand when she was pregnant! *Call me.*"

Auwe. I decided to wait until I got home to call her back, then wondered if I should swing by to see her instead on my way.

I figured I should also check in with Summer, since my next move might be a long-shot trip to Maui and I'd be consuming more of her retainer. I dialed her Kāhala number and got that foreign voice on the machine again. "Leave message at tone . . ."

"Summer, I've made some progress but may need to fly to Maui to follow up on a lead. It's Wednesday afternoon at four. Please let me hear from you by tonight, either at my office or at home."

That evening I arrived at Ah Fook in Chinatown before Tommy Woo did. Inside the dinky chop sui house there was no place to wait for a cramped table except behind the swinging glass door, and I didn't want to stand there. So I joined the line of a half dozen customers outside on infamous River Street, where colorful thieves, con artists, drug runners, and occasional murderers once plied their dark trades.

Ah Fook's best-kept secret was a fancy menu for such a funky place: Shark Fin Soup, Stuffed Clams with Crab Meat, Peking Duck Dim Sum. Regular customers like Tommy and me never praised Ah Fook, for fear it would be overrun. Instead we embellished its deplorable reputation (which had some slim basis in fact): cockroaches roaming the walls, ants crawling on the tables, dog meat in the pork fried rice, payoffs to the health department and liquor commission.

Tommy was coming from a rehearsal for one of his jazz gigs and warned me he might be late. How he managed to wrap up a late-night session at 2:00 a.m., then cruise into his legal offices—eyes wide open—by eight the next morning is anybody's guess.

I checked my watch—ten after seven—just as a familiar dark profile emerged from the night and joined me at the front of the lengthening line.

"Hey, Kai, what do you call a guy who hangs out with musicians?"

Tommy Woo always wore black and always had a joke on the tip of his tongue. Over my shoulder I scanned the waiting customers lining River Street for ears that might be too tender or young for one of Tommy's doozies.

"Cooke, party of two." Fortunately, the hostess stepped out and led us inside. Our cramped corner table was so close to our fellow diners that I could smell their perfume and aftershave, but it was thankfully too loud inside the tiny restaurant to distinguish their words. A dozen animated conversations bouncing off the walls drowned out one another, making Ah Fook an unexpectedly intimate place.

I watched my friend's loose-jointed and lanky form squeeze behind the tiny round table. Divorced, pushing fifty, with a shock of grey hair and tortoise shell glasses, Tommy resembled a cross between a parish priest and Yo-Yo Ma. An only child, his father had been Chinese, his mother Jewish, he attended Catholic schools, and was exposed from infancy to the jazz and blues of Duke Ellington, Charlie Parker, and B.B. King. Tommy Woo had the wisdom of Confucius, the funny bone of a rabbi, the pomp and circumstance of the Pope, and the musical soul of an African. He could spin ethnic and off-color yarns until your face turned blue, then thrill and inspire you at the piano with "Take the 'A' Train" and "Body and Soul."

"*A drummer,*" Tommy uttered while taking his seat. "That's what they call a guy who hangs out with musicians."

"Oh." I scratched my head at the tamest tale Tommy had ever told. "You must not think much of drummers, I guess."

"Actually, I do." Tommy cracked a wry smile. "Good ones."

After two more of Tommy's salty and unrepeatable humdingers, we ordered the usual—the $8.95 dinner special: Egg Drop Soup, Sweet-Sour Spareribs, Shrimp Fried Rice,

Lemon Chicken, Fortune Cookie (a rarity in Honolulu), and hot tea. The tea arrived almost instantly.

"So what's new with your practice, Tommy?"

"Jus' laugh'n 'n scratch'n," he joked. "Actually, I'm defending a mainland guy who sold some ice to an undercover cop. The narcs were laying a trap for the Sun organization, and my client—who has no connection to Frank O. Sun—got busted. He comes from a good family, has a good job here, and has never been arrested. Just thought he'd try a little meth on a lark. Then he got engaged to a nice local girl who reviles drug users and he tried to recoup his investment by selling the stuff to some other sucker."

"He should have flushed it down the toilet." I shook my head as the Egg Drop Soup arrived. "Do you expect a judge to believe him?"

Tommy sipped the hot soup and shrugged. "No, the narcs want to make an example of him."

"Frank O. Sun. What's his story? I've heard the name."

"Sun?" Tommy brushed back his shock of grey hair. "He comes from nowhere and everywhere. He's ubiquitous, my lad, *ubiquitous.* He wears his trademark Panama hat and sunglasses—always—day and night. Some say he's Korean, others that he's German or Bolivian. I doubt his real name is Sun. It may be *Sonne*—German, you know. But no one of my acquaintance has actually seen him in the flesh."

"Ubiquitous, huh?" I tried on Tommy's big word.

"Sun has a fairly complex organization of suppliers, distributors, dealers, money launderers, strong arms—the whole tamale. His group reaches from the islands to the Orient, California, and into Mexico and South America. Sun Imports, his front business, is a warehouse off Ward Avenue. The place has atmosphere—straw on the floor and steamer trunks full of pottery and exotic foreign goods. It's a popular store."

"I've seen it, just never dropped in."

"You're not the pottery type, Kai." Tommy grinned. "Neither am I."

The waitress brought our ribs and fried rice. Tommy went first for the meat. "And what these days occupies the Surfing Detective?"

We switched serving plates. "Another crazy case." I said. "This California blonde—very pregnant—who'll only meet at Denny's in Waikīkī. No explanation why. She's gorgeous, though. Never mind she looks as if she could give birth to a baby whale at any moment."

"So what does this pregnant woman want with you?"

"She wants me to prove her husband is dead."

"She doesn't know if her own husband is dead?"

"It's a life insurance claim for two hundred grand."

"Ah." Tommy nodded knowingly. "That ought to make her comfortable for a while."

I gave him the brief version of Corky's wipeout and the red flags that the insurance company was balking at.

"Any question in your mind that this surfer is dead?"

"If Corky was planning to skip, he couldn't have done a better job of preparing his nest egg: empty bank accounts, maxed-out credit cards, a missing BMW. But, except for a sliced surfboard leash, there's no real evidence. And I doubt he and the wife are in this together. I'd say she's a victim of her husband's irresponsibility."

The Lemon Chicken arrived, followed by more hot tea.

"By the way," Tommy asked idly, "what motive would your surfer have to skip?"

"To escape fatherhood, to keep on surfing free. That's the best I can come up with. But no way could he ever become the sponsored, big name surfer he dreamed of—not without his wife and the insurance company finding out. So what's the point in skipping?"

When our fortune cookies finally appeared, neither made sense to us, but they rarely do. My "An exotic companion awaits you" was at least more intriguing than solo Tommy's: "Family always comes first."

Later that night, back at the Waikīkī Edgewater, there were no messages waiting for me—not from Summer or Leimomi. Then I remembered, too late, that I had promised to call Lei. Once again, that unflattering parallel between Corky and me came to mind.

eleven

I didn't sleep well that night and awoke Thursday morning with a groggy head, fuzzy mouth, and a feeling of dread. The case was on my mind. So was Leimomi.

I flipped through the wad of green hundreds. A flight to Maui and a rental car for the day would cost less than a few bills. Hardly a dent.

Two people had told me that Maya was from Maui. And one of them had a hazy recollection that she'd resided upcountry in Makawao. If these tips turned out to be true, it shouldn't be hard to find her in the small mountain town. A few sloping blocks of wood frame buildings comprised the main drag of this commercial and cultural hub of upcountry Maui. Makawao could be canvassed easily in a few hours. I would have liked to discuss the trip with Summer first. But since she wasn't returning my calls, I might as well just *holoholo*.

The Aloha 737 quickly left Oʻahu behind on this cloudless winter morning, crossed the wind-whipped channel to Molokaʻi, then skirted the sloping red plateau of its west end.

Across from Moloka'i lay the tiny island of Lāna'i, the rural and remote Pineapple Isle, which is dominated by a three-thousand-foot volcano, Lāna'ihale.

The jet glided over cane fields on the isthmus between Maui's twin volcanic cones and touched down at Kahului Airport at ten, leaving me the better part of the day to poke around. The sub-compact I had reserved from Dollar was sold out, so at no extra charge they gave me a silver-blue Mercury Grand Marquis, whose overstuffed leather seats could have accommodated Summer's whole crew of dark escorts.

I pulled away from the airport and cruised toward Upcountry Maui, turning onto Baldwin Avenue at the former bustling sugar town of Pā'ia. Dubbed "noisy" in plantation times, today this rustic country town hosted quieter tourism. As the Grand Marquis climbed Baldwin past a rusting sugar mill and, by contrast, spotlessly white churches, the shoulderless road twisted higher into wide-open acres, ranches, and secluded luxury homes. The Mercury leaned precariously around each hairpin turn, as the mountain air grew cooler and more fragrant. It smelled pine fresh up here. High-country fresh.

Along with Kamuela on the Big Island, Makawao was one of the islands' last genuine cowboy towns and it looked the part: Old West wood-frame buildings with hitching posts recalled John Wayne movies. Settled near the end of the 19th century by Portuguese immigrants who raised cattle on upcountry slopes, this former rough and tumble mountain hamlet today boasts an eclectic blend of western, *paniolo*, Yuppie, New Age, and alternative. You can buy a saddle, have your palm read, attend a rodeo, order a veggie burger, and watch a glass blower. All in the same little town.

What did Makawao's character say about Maya? Was this North Shore surfer girl also a cowgirl or a hippie? An artsy type? A vegetarian? I aimed to find out.

Near the corner of Makawao and Baldwin Avenues, I stepped into a New Age bookshop called Om, where the musty smell of incense hit me like a wall. Besides herbal essences, bath oils, and scented candles, there were also a few books and tapes and CDs, most of the occult, astrological, and inspirational variety. Airy space music—from a group called Cosmic Tofu, said the display—wafted through the haze. *Tommy Woo would cringe.*

A wispy brunette, gold ring dangling from her nose, greeted me with penetrating cobalt-blue eyes that made me feel naked.

"How are *you* today?" she asked, sounding like she actually wanted to hear my answer.

"I have a favor to ask."

Her blue eyes didn't blink.

"I'm looking for someone named Maya—tall, red hair, maybe from around here. I don't have her picture, but I do have her boyfriend's." I showed her Corky's youthful face.

"Too bad he's taken." She studied the photo intently. "And you say his partner's name is Maya?"

"Right."

"You don't have a last name?"

I shrugged. "I know it's a long shot . . ."

She shook her head. "I really wish I could help." She sounded sincerely sorry.

"Where else would somebody who lives around here shop?"

"Paniolo Trading Company. And the natural foods stores—there are two—one on Makawao, one on Baldwin."

"She would need groceries, that's for sure. Thanks." I turned and left her behind in the incense haze.

Whole Earth Foods was just next door. But no one there had heard of Maya or recognized Corky. At Ambrosia, the second health food store on Baldwin Avenue, I did no better. Next I tried an antique shop and an adjacent real estate office. Same drill. Same response.

Trying not to lose hope, I stepped across Baldwin Avenue onto the plank boardwalk fronting the Paniolo Trading Company, whose rippled tin awning offered welcome shade as the scorching sun pierced thin mountain air. The old-fashioned general store smelled of roasting turkey and saddle leather and motor oil. This place had everything someone in a small cowboy town might need, from Band-Aids to videos to fresh *ahi*. Even an ATM machine. And, of course, Jim Beam. But no one I talked to knew of Maya or had seen a mug like Corky's— except in the Honolulu papers.

Bummahs. By now it was well after noon and everybody in Makawao was eating lunch except me. I found a yuppie deli tucked between some artsy shops in a courtyard shaded by a *hau* tree. I ordered a seared *ahi* croissant (the closest they had to a sandwich) and a Coke, hoping the caffeine and sugar might stimulate some new thought on the case.

Sitting under the hau's spreading boughs, I scanned the surrounding shops and wondered if Maya might patronize any of them: a seascape gallery, a second-hand boutique selling granny dresses and *da kine*, a jeweler specializing in sterling silver, and a glass blower.

I doubted if Maya had ongoing use for a glass blower, but it looked like the most interesting of the shops. I finished my *ahi* and wandered inside. The blower was hard at work. A molten orange blob at the end of his long tube glowed like fiery lava. As he turned it round and round, the orange glow became a perfect crystal sphere—evidently a paperweight, as the nearby shelves displayed. Brilliant orbs, they glinted with vibrant colors—turquoise, pumpkin, scarlet, saffron, peach.

I lifted up one in apple green, the size of a baseball. Sticker shock! It cost as much as the tab for this whole trip.

"That's one of our most popular crystals," said a woman with frosted hair who had crept up behind me. "Lovely, isn't it?"

"I might have to hock my car to buy it," I joked.

"We have a layaway plan," she said with a straight face. "The smaller weights are less."

In spite of myself, I checked one in ocean blue the size of an Easter egg. Inside the crystal were delicate turquoise-tinted swirls like undulating waves. It was beautiful. And only half the price of the larger green one. I wondered if Leimomi would like it.

"You can almost see the ocean inside, can't you?" the woman purred.

You could. On an extravagant whim, I replied: "I'll take this one for my girlfriend."

"She'll love it."

Then I pulled out Corky's photo. "I'm looking for an old friend named Maya who may be with this man. I can give you his name if that would help."

"I don't need his name," she said proudly. "He looks different without his beard, of course, but I would recognize that boyish face and those green eyes anywhere. That's Charles, Maya's husband."

"Yes." I tried not to betray myself.

"They were in last week. Maya bought a crystal vase for their cottage. I think they're renting. Just moved in about a month ago."

"Is it near town?"

"You can't miss it—the yellow one about a mile down the road."

I thanked her, paid for the crystal orb, and headed to my waiting Mercury.

She was right. The yellow cottage wasn't hard to find. Beyond the weathered tombstones of St. Joseph's Catholic Church, it sat just outside of town among velvet green horse pastures. I pulled into a gravel drive and walked up to the tin-roofed cottage. The place looked deserted.

"Hello, anybody home?" I said through a screen door.

No one answered.

"Hello?"

No response.

I peeked in the mailbox and I found a phone bill addressed to "Maya Livengood," and a letter forwarded from Kē Nui Road—also in her name. There was a third forwarded letter addressed to "Charles McDahl" that was postmarked January third—over a month ago—in Lewiston, Idaho, but just forwarded a few days past. The handwriting looked feminine and shaky. And the sender's last name was the same as Corky's. Maybe his mother?

Tampering with U.S. Mail was a federal offense, punishable by serious jail time. A PI could lose his license. I stuffed the letter in my pocket. Climbing into the Grand Marquis, I aimed down the gravel drive and headed back to Kahului Airport.

twelve

Until my Honolulu-bound jetliner was wheels up and climbing, I resisted opening the envelope. The letter was written in the same feminine shaky hand.

Dear Charles,

Son, thank God you are alive! The story of your surfing accident at Waimea Bay was carried on all the TV networks and CNN, on the radio, and even the Lewiston paper. They all believed you were dead. But I prayed to God that you survived. My prayers have been answered.

It's a shame you have to hide from those bad men and can't even let your wife know you are alive. I fully understand and will keep your secret.

Please send me your new address.

Love,

Mom

Corky was more of a fool than I had imagined. If you are planning to disappear, the last person on earth you want to tell is your own mother. Any halfway decent insurance investigator would start with her. If Mr. Gold had not, he wasn't doing his job. But, then, if he had, maybe this mother who wasn't bright enough leave her fleeing son's name off envelopes *was* bright enough to fool an insurance investigator.

I returned to Maunakea Street late that afternoon, letter in hand—my only piece of hard evidence that Corky McDahl was apparently very much alive.

Mr. Gold had good reason to be suspicious. But I wasn't working for Mr. Gold. I was working for Summer, who was now more mysterious to me than ever. Was she totally in the dark, as the letter suggested? Or was she working with Corky? And perhaps Maya? And who were these "bad men"—the same men with Summer in the black Mercedes? Or were the "bad men" just some excuse Corky had given his mother to justify his running out on his pregnant wife and taking up with another woman?

The red light on my answering machine reminded me that Summer had never returned my call. I pressed Play and heard Tommy Woo's voice.

"Hey, Kai, did you hear the one about the Chinese, Filipino, and Hawaiian astronauts . . ." After a punch line that would get Tommy himself punched in some circles, he added "My client got hung out to dry by the Sun organization. He took the rap for that ice he sold. Thought you'd like to know."

Why did Tommy think I would like to know? Because the same thing had happened to Leimomi's father, who was still cooling his heels in prison? Her dad could have plea-bargained for a lighter sentence, and been out by now on parole, had he testified against the kingpin. But that meant harassment, bodily harm, or death.

As I erased Tommy's message, there was a gentle *tap . . . tap . . . tap* at my door. I reached for the knob and found Leimomi standing there, still wearing her *lei* stringing clothes—white Bermudas and a pink T-shirt that said "Fujiyama's Flower Lei's" and carried the ambrosial scent of ginger and *pīkake*. I glanced involuntarily at her tummy, wondering if it had already started to bulge like Summer's.

"I'm worried, Kai."

I took her warm hand and walked her to my client's chair. "Sit down and tell me what's happening."

"Nothing's changed," she said looking distracted. "Nothing at all has changed."

"Tomorrow's Friday." I tried to cheer her up. "Let's go out to dinner and have a relaxing evening together. It might do you good. Pick you up at seven?"

"A nice dinner won't change anything. It will be the same problem tomorrow."

"Wait and see. Here . . ." I pulled a twenty from my wallet. "Why don't you buy one of those test kits and then you'll know for sure."

"What if I don't want to know?"

"Leimomi . . ." The next hour was spent talking in circles, with Leimomi crying, me consoling, and nothing getting resolved. After she left, I realized I had completely forgotten about the ocean blue crystal egg I had bought for her. *Auwe!*

I tried calling Summer later and was surprised when she actually answered.

"What evidence have you found?" she asked matter-of-factly. There was a coolness and distance I hadn't heard before.

"I've found evidence, but not that Corky died."

"What do you mean?" She sounded curious, but not ecstatic.

"If you are not sitting down, Summer, I suggest you do."

"I'm already sitting. What is it?"

"Corky may be alive."

Silence.

"I've just come from upcountry Maui where he is most likely staying with a friend."

"What friend? He doesn't have any friends there."

"I'm not sure," I lied. She didn't need to be told just yet that not only had her husband faked his own death and skipped out on her, but also was living with another woman. Or maybe it was Summer who should be telling *me* these things.

"I want to see you," she said suddenly. "I want to see this evidence."

"OK. But let's meet in my office. The evidence is confidential and I don't want to carry it out of here."

"Alright." She agreed. "When?"

It was nearly four. "Can you get over here by 4:30?"

There was a long pause, as if she were consulting someone. "Yes. How do I get there?"

I gave her directions, then hung up the phone. I tilted back in my swivel chair, feet up on the desk, and puzzled over my client and her husband and his redhead girlfriend. Love triangle? Co-conspirators? At this point, the jury was still out.

Suddenly I got chicken skin—goose bumps—as if surfing in wintry conditions without a wetsuit. I took my feet off the desk and opened its wide center drawer.

Way in back under a tablet of yellow legal paper lay my Smith & Wesson. The blue-black .357 Magnum felt cold and heavy in my hands. It was loaded with six rounds. I put it on one corner of my desktop, artfully covered with a loose arrangement of bills and receipts I had neglected to file.

I put the letter from Corky's mother under the plastic liner in my wastebasket. If Summer decided to bring company, I didn't want anybody to walk off with it.

The longer I thought about my client's visit, the more uneasy I felt. On impulse I called Tommy.

thirteen

"Hey, Kai," Tommy answered on the second ring, "Did you hear the one about the curvy local girl who went door-to-door as a handy-man?"

"Can the jokes, Tommy," I cut him off. "I've got a quick favor to ask."

"Shoot."

"Somebody's coming to my office at four thirty and I'm a little concerned—not about her—but about who she might bring along."

"The pregnant blonde? The wife of the dead California surfer?"

"He's not dead. He's living in upcountry Maui with his new girlfriend."

"So he skipped out after all." Tommy didn't sound surprised.

"Looks like it, but there may be another angle. I'm wondering if the wife is caught up in something much larger."

"Yeah? Well, what can I do for you, Kai?"

"She's coming at four thirty . . . Would you call me at quarter to five? Just to see if I'm still breathing?"

"Sure."

"Thanks." I checked my desk clock. "She'll be here any minute. Talk with you later."

I hung up and waited. If Summer stayed true to form, she would show up at least ten minutes late. I should have told Tommy to call at five.

At 4:25 a faint knock sounded at my door. Before I could reach the knob, the solid mahogany swung open to reveal two men in black suits. No Summer.

One of the men had dark hair and complexion, maybe Middle Eastern or Mediterranean. I recognized him as Summer's escort. The other had bleached white hair and the washed-out skin of an albino. The whites of his eyes were a mouse-like pink. This odd pair of men stood in my doorway, silently—me looking at them, them looking at me.

"Mr. Cooke?" The dark man broke the silence. He didn't look angry or belligerent. He actually cracked a smile—which worried me.

"Yes, I'm Kai Cooke."

He reached into his pocket. I edged toward the Smith & Wesson. If he was pulling out his piece, I wanted mine too.

"'Gratulation!" blurted the white-haired one. Then his partner handed me a wad of green bills—Ben Franklins—rolled cylindrically like *sushi,* with money where the rice and Spam would go, and bound by a rubber band.

"Mr. Sun say investigation over," announced the white one.

"Mr. Sun? But Summer . . ."

"No, sir," said the dark one in the accent of an English gentleman. "You are under the employ of Mr. Frank O. Sun. And when Mr. Sun says your investigation is over, Mr. Sun means your investigation is over. *Understood, sir?*"

"Sure, I understand." It appeared there was only one right answer.

"Thank you, then," the dark one replied. "We bid you good day, sir." They headed out the door.

"Wait"—I tried to stop them—"Summer . . ." The door was shut on my words.

The roll of hundreds in my hand began to feel heavy. I set it on my desk and slumped into my padded chair. I was gazing at the ceiling when my phone rang.

"You OK, Kai?" It was Tommy.

"Yeah, I'm OK. Tell me about Frank O. Sun."

"Is that who she brought?"

"Summer didn't show. Just two extremely well-dressed gentlemen—*malahinis*—who dropped several grand into my hands and told me to stop my investigation. They said *Mr. Sun* wanted me to stop."

"Drugs," Tommy said, "or drug money. Those are the only things that move Frank O. Sun."

"But how does Summer fit into this?" I wondered aloud. "She might be in danger."

"Or she might be pulling the wool over your eyes," Tommy smirked. "I've always thought you're too much of a choir boy to be a private dick."

"Help me think here, Tommy. Could Corky be connected to Sun? What would a surfer do for a drug lord?"

"Who knows? Sun has a big organization . . ." Tommy was silent for a rare moment. "You said your surfer made lots of trips between California and Hawai'i. Did he ever surf in Mexico? Maybe he's a small-time supplier, or a dealer, or a mule."

"Then what about Summer?"

"Maybe Sun couldn't find him and had her hire you to do it for him, which means Sun wants this Corky *badly.* He probably skipped out with cash or drugs."

"And a BMW convertible."

"That too. I would guess if they get to him before you do, he's toast."

"Not good."

"Why should you care about him?"

"I don't. I'm just worried about his pregnant wife if Sun has her. Once he deals with Corky, what value is she?"

"You really think she's not involved?"

"I think she's innocent."

"You might be surprised, my friend."

Tommy's words rang in my ears after he hung up.

fourteen

Removing the rubber band from the green roll on my desk, I peeled off one bill after another. These were not crisp new notes, but well worn, high-mileage currency that had wandered the streets.

I counted to fifteen and still had more than half the roll left. Then I wrapped the loose bills back into the wad, and slipped it into my desk's top drawer, by the Smith & Wesson.

I decided to leave a message for Summer. I made it brief: "Summer, please call me if you need further assistance."

I didn't really expect to hear from her. She was spinning in Sun's powerful orbit; who was I to pull her out? Tommy was very likely right. I had been merely an errand boy—and now Mr. Sun was through with me. I wasn't going to give up, but I did take his message seriously. A shadowy drug lord was often a businessman of many enterprises.

My job now was to find Summer's wayward husband before Sun did, if it meant saving her. I wondered if Sun's men would stop tailing me just because my investigation had been declared over.

I locked the two dead bolts of my door on my way out, then navigated the incense haze wafting from Madame Zenobia's shop. Descending the stairs I spotted Leimomi in the back room stringing blue-dyed carnations and perfumy tuberose. *Tourist lei.* She sat by herself, looking glum, so I rushed on before she could catch my eye. But I didn't evade Mrs. Fujiyama.

"Mr. Cooke." Her courteous smile straightened.

"Hello, Mrs. Fujiyama. How are you today?"

"Very good," said the silver-haired matriarch. "But not so good my *lei* girl."

"Anything wrong?" I acted puzzled, but a sinking feeling told me what my landlady was about to say.

"Leimomi." Mrs. Fujiyama's smile now turned down at the corners.

"What's wrong?" I asked the obvious.

"Maybe *you* know?" She peered at me over her half glasses. "You her friend, yes?"

"Yes, I'm her friend . . ." What else could I say? *She thinks she's pregnant and I'm the father?* That wouldn't do. So I settled for, "We're having dinner tonight. I could ask her then if anything's wrong."

"Leimomi very young." Mrs. Fujiyama's eyes darkened.

"Yes, Leimomi is young," I conceded.

"Time for Mr. Cooke to marry?" She held me in her gaze. "Maybe you like have family—wife and *keiki*. Single life not so good, you know."

"Plenty of time," I said uncomfortably. "I'm only thirty-four."

"Thirty-four," she echoed. "Old man already. You be surprise'. Time fly. Before you know it—too old for family. Wife want young man. Not dry old man."

I was about to say something I'd probably regret, so I let her remark pass and made for the door.

Later that afternoon I headed for a quick session at Paradise. There was still one hour of light. I intended to use it.

Off shore of the Halekūlani Hotel, Paradise is one of the most remote and least crowded spots in Waikīkī, producing a narrow, peaky break that pumps up into crystal-blue curls. Takeoffs are steep and lightning fast. Rides are brief and intense. Though compared to the liquid mountains I had scaled at Waimea Bay, these small swells were tiny anthills.

But today I had them nearly to myself—one pristine swell after another—since most dedicated surfers were still haunting the North Shore. At the first glimmers of sunset, the sweet strains of an 'ukulele and the twang of a slack key guitar from the Halekūlani echoed across the water. The spendthrift setting sun painted the sky with more gold than all the kings and queens of the world ever owned.

Out here I felt immeasurably rich. Out here I felt at peace. But back on shore trouble was brewing.

Friday morning I flew to Maui for the second time in less than twenty-four hours. On the plane in first class sat a pale, white-haired man in dark glasses looking eerily similar to Sun's albino. I watched him disembark at Kahului Airport, then waited until he had claimed his luggage and hailed a taxi before I picked up my rental car.

Find Corky first. That's what ran through my mind as the grey Nissan climbed twisting Baldwin Avenue into the cool upcountry. I glanced again and again in the rear view mirrors. Nothing but winding road.

Soon the eclectic town of Makawao came into view. Today I bypassed the general store and the New Age book shop, and drove straight to the yellow cottage. It hadn't changed since yesterday. The overgrown cane field—stray stalks bending forlornly—still climbed the sloping hillside beyond it. I knocked on the screen door.

"Anyone home?"

No answer, though the inner door was open and what I saw inside didn't look right.

"Hello?" I knocked again and waited.

No reply.

The screen door made a chilling squeal when I pulled it open. The cottage was in shambles. Either Corky and his lady friend lived like pigs, or they had been visited by pigs. Papers and magazines were scattered on the floor. A wastebasket was overturned. Unwashed dishes filled the sink. On the dining table, breakfast sat uneaten: two bowls of cereal soggy in milk, a glass of orange juice in which floated a drowned fly, and a full cup of coffee. One of the chairs had been turned over on its side; another, pushed back far from the table, tilted rakishly against the sink counter. From the look of this barely touched breakfast, someone had evidently split in a hurry.

I walked to the one and only bedroom, where a similar disorder prevailed. A double bed with sheets and blankets ripped off revealed a naked mattress stained in suggestive places. Dresser drawers lay open and emptied onto the floor. Bikini panties and jockey shorts were strewn and draped about.

I peered out a back window. After the mayhem in the cottage, the tidy rows of young salad greens in a vegetable garden struck me as odd.

"Anybody home?" I said a little louder than before.

Still no answer.

I wandered out into the yard and toward the overgrown cane field. And there, at the edge of the property where a split-rail fence separated a shaggy lawn from the field, stood a tall redhead whose hair glowed like copper wire in the morning sun. Her long slender arms were spread wide on the top rail resembling wings. She was gazing straight down at her feet. Her stance almost cut the figure of a crucifix: forlorn, solemn.

"Hello?" I edged toward her.

Her head slowly rose and turned in my direction. She had the face of a boy—a handsome, animated, sad boy. Grey-green eyes contrasted her copper hair. Rainbow-colored love beads hung around her neck. She wore faded denim bellbottoms and a scarlet tie-dyed T-shirt that revealed the silhouette of bare breasts.

"I'm looking for a Charles McDahl." I moved in for closer inspection. "Have you seen him?"

Her sad face, up close, was lightly freckled and a little less boyish. Fine, delicate lines around her eyes recalled Skipper's observation that Corky's "lady friend" was several years his senior. Maybe she actually *was* a child of the sixties.

"You're looking for Corky?" she replied in the high, husky tones of an adolescent whose voice is changing. "He's out there."

She pointed to the fallow field. There was a faraway look in her eyes. "They just left. They took him into that field. Except the older man. He stayed in the car."

"Frank O. Sun?"

"I don't know." She glanced away. "They kept me in the cottage. I heard a pop. Then they drove off."

She turned her distant eyes on me. "I'm Maya, Corky's wife." She offered me her fine-boned hand.

"Kai Cooke. I'm a private investigator." As my own hand closed over hers, I tried not to look too astonished at her declaration. Corky now had two widows?

When she began climbing over the split-rail fence, I followed her. She didn't try to stop me. I noticed she was in fact wearing a band on her ring finger, though dull like brass rather than gleaming like gold. We stepped warily through the uncultivated fields, searching the sod for what seemed inevitable.

"What did the men want from Corky?" I asked as gently as I could.

She didn't answer, just scanned the barren ground. Then she stopped and turned to me. She had begun to cry.

"They just kept shouting at him," she said through her tears. "'Where is it? Where is it?' . . . Everybody shouting . . ."

She started to walk away again, her steps now a stagger.

"Can you remember what the men looked like?" I tried another question, but too late.

Maya had frozen in place, suddenly silent and pale. I followed her gaze to the shallow ravine ahead of her.

fifteen

The red earth was stained black with blood. The biggest stain formed a ragged circle the size of a car wheel. Smaller spots dotted a meandering path. It looked as if someone had been shot and then dragged away. *He bled profusely,* I said only to myself. *They must have shot him point-blank.*

Maya mechanically followed the trail of blood, heading in the direction of the yellow cottage. Part way there, she bent down to pick up a black rubber *zori*. It was large and a local brand—"Surfah."

"His slipper," Maya said without emotion. "That's Corky's slipper."

She then picked up a pair of mirrored sunglasses that even I recognized. In the photo that Summer had given me, hanging around Corky's neck by thick cords was this same pair—the expensive kind some surfers wear. Surfers with money.

I figured the body of Corky McDahl was probably riding in the trunk of a car at this very moment, or his remains had already been dumped in an upcountry field or into the ocean.

I turned to Maya. "It looks like they took him away," I said in the most innocuous way I could. "It looks like they removed him from the scene."

She didn't respond but kept walking toward the cottage. I wondered why Sun had left Maya behind alive. She knew of Corky's dealings with Sun, I would bet, and now she could identify the men who'd taken him, if not Sun himself.

"Can you think of what they might have wanted from Corky?" I asked her again as I opened the screen door. Maya walked ahead of me, then stopped at the sight of the half-eaten breakfast. She ran her spider-like fingers through her hair and then looked up and studied my face for a long time. She appeared to be weighing my trustworthiness.

"It would help with the investigation," I coaxed her gently. "I wouldn't want you to be next."

Maya righted the tilted chair and slumped down into it. "Corky worked for a man in California named Damon," she began hesitantly, "Damon DiCarlo. At first Corky just took care of his BMW, but then DiCarlo said he would give Corky the car if he helped ship it to Honolulu. All Corky had to do was pick it up at the boat dock in Honolulu—and it was his."

"After Sun removed the drugs?" I helped her story along.

"Ice." Maya nodded. "Forty pounds hidden in the car."

"That's what, a million in street value?"

"I guess. But Sun never got it. Corky picked up the car at Sand Island and drove off."

"Was he *crazy?*"

"Corky had it in for DiCarlo, not Sun. He never intended to deliver his car, or the ice, once he found out DiCarlo was sleeping with his wife."

"His wife?" I stared. "But you said . . ."

"Yeah, Corky and I really are married. And he's still married to her too." Maya said this with a weird kind of distance. "But her baby's not Corky's. It's DiCarlo's."

"What? Is that what Corky told you?"

"When Summer got pregnant she wanted Corky to bring home more money, so he agreed to ship DiCarlo's car."

"And DiCarlo is a supplier for Frank O. Sun."

"Yeah, he brings drugs from Mexico into California and then ships them to Hawai'i. Corky hid the ice, sold the car, and faked his wipeout at Waimea Bay," Maya said matter-of-factly. "We hid out on the North Shore for a while, then on Lāna'i, now here."

"Where is the ice?"

"On O'ahu. Corky didn't tell me where exactly—to protect me."

"Or it was to protect him?" I said. "I'm sure you've thought of this, but what makes you think he wasn't going to skip out on you too?"

Maya seemed unfazed. "Then why would he tell me about the map he drew to the very spot?"

"There's a map?" Her story was getting loonier by the minute.

"On Lāna'i."

I figured she was either setting me up for a really wild goose chase, or this was the key to the whole thing. "Then I guess we better get ourselves over to Lāna'i and find that map before Sun does."

"Go to Lāna'i? Now?" Maya's freckled brow furrowed. "Give me a minute." She disappeared into her bedroom.

I considered phoning the Maui police, but decided against it. We couldn't afford the time for police reports and the interrogations that always follow a murder. Maya herself, as Corky's girlfriend—or "wife"—would be a crucial witness to his death, if not a suspect. And without her, even the tiny island of Lānaʻi would seem like a huge place to hunt for one solitary map.

A few minutes later Maya emerged with a small duffle slung over her shoulder. Her sad face now showed an eerily vacant smile. Her hippie look had been replaced by Hawaiian chic: a hibiscus print sundress in blood red that echoed her fiery hair. The neckline was cut tantalizingly low, and she hadn't bothered to wear a bra. It was easy to see how Corky might have been drawn in by Maya's seemingly unconscious sexuality. She had a gypsy, footloose quality about her that seemed to lure one on an exotic journey.

But even though she lived up to everybody's intoxicating description, her empty smile so soon after the murder did make me leery of her. *What is this woman made of?* Was Maya simply trying to make the best of a traumatic event? Or was she traumatized herself— her face a plaster mask reflecting the numbness that covers pain?

Maya slipped into the front seat of my rental car and we pulled away. With her sitting so close to me in that splashy red dress, it was a chore keeping the Nissan on Maui's twisting roads. But I did. All the way back to Kahului Airport.

sixteen

By mid-morning we were airborne to Lāna'i. Cotton candy clouds floated lazily above the pitched roof of Lāna'ihale. Maya held onto her seat and her vacant smile as the Twin Otter shuddered through the clouds, then swept over Lāna'i's towering sea cliffs to a tiny asphalt strip.

Dwarf *kiawe* dotted the plains beneath us where pineapple once grew, the *kiawe's* ashen, salt-bitten stalks rolling endlessly up to the horizon. Atop a distant slope, Norfolk pines marked off Lāna'i City and the grand sprawling Lodge at Koele.

The Twin Otter bounced twice on the slender strip before settling into an even roll. At the cozy little airport on the Pineapple Isle you can't hire a rental car; you must catch a shuttle bus upslope to Lāna'i City. We hopped off the Otter and onto the bus. The shuttle climbed the slanting plateau toward those statuesque Norfolk pines, providing sweeping views of the small island.

Given my hurry to find that map, I was glad of these visual reminders that the teardrop-shaped island of Lāna'i stretches only about eighteen miles by a dozen. The austere, bone-grey landscape brought to mind Hawaiian legend portraying this as a forlorn, desolate place haunted by the spirits of buried *ali'i* and, therefore, uninhabitable by mortal beings. Although since the 1990s two elegant resorts—the Mānele Bay and the Lodge at Koele—have combined to employ more workers than did the nation's largest pineapple plantation here.

The shuttle climbed slowly toward Lāna'i City—too slowly for me. We didn't have endless time. Sun would soon enough figure out, if he hadn't already, that I had with me the only person other than Corky McDahl who could lead him to his stash. Maya wasn't saying much about the missing ice, or her departed lover, though she spoke freely enough about herself through that eerie smile that hadn't left her face since we left Maui.

Maya was forty-six. She told me this with pride, since she apparently knew she looked ten years younger. A military kid, born "Mary Leavis" to an artillery captain and a nightclub dancer in Texas, she grew up in the sixties bouncing from base to base. She later married and divorced twice, then changed her name to "Maya Livengood" when she became a free spirit in Hawai'i, drifting from island to island. Since then she had occupied herself swimming and diving and haunting the beaches of Hawai'i's famous breaks—and hooking up with guys like Corky who surfed them. To hear her tell it, she relished her mellow footloose lifestyle.

"I'm into astrology," Maya announced, with an artful flutter of her long eyelashes. "That's how I knew Corky and I were right for each other. We were both water signs. He was a Pisces—a fish. And I'm a Cancer—a crab. His wife was all wrong for him. She's an earth sign—Virgo the virgin—too distant and proper for a fluid, free-wheeling Pisces." She looked at me intently. "What's your sign, Kai?"

"No signs for me, thanks. Whatever my horoscope says, I'm sure I don't want to know."

"You're bull-headed." Maya shook her long hair. "What are you, a Taurus?"

"You missed my point, entirely."

She got quiet again. But that ghost of a smile didn't leave her face.

The shuttle bus crested the rise into Lāna'i City—sixteen hundred feet above sea level—where the pines pointed into the sky like giant green arrows. The stately evergreens lent the plantation town an air of mountain serenity and coolness. Surrounded by these soaring Norfolks, grassy Dole Park lay at center of the village. A bank, a general store, a few diners, and other small businesses sat on the park's perimeter with rustic sun-faded facades suggesting an earlier era. The village's nearly deserted streets reinforced the sense of desolation that had set in at the airport.

We stepped off the shuttle by the kelly green Lāna'i Plantation Store, whose red tin roof covered gas pumps, a small convenience store, and the island's only car rental agency.

"It's time you told me," I said, opening the store's door. "Where's the map hidden?"

Maya didn't hesitate. "On Shipwreck Beach."

"Shipwreck Beach? That's eight miles of sand and junk."

"Corky told me the map is inside a sunscreen bottle."

"Eight miles, and we're looking for one sunscreen bottle?" I couldn't help but sound exasperated.

"There's more . . ." Maya paused. "Corky told me to walk the beach to that stranded Navy ship—the huge one that ran aground offshore."

"That narrows it down some," I said, a trace of exasperation still in my voice.

By noon Maya and I were twisting down the sun-bleached highway to Shipwreck Beach in a Jeep Wrangler—rear-view mirrors, for the moment, empty. A conventional car would have done us little good on this rugged island, whose roads other than this narrow paved highway were mostly sand and dirt and mud. Soon we would need all four wheels pulling.

The road wove down six miles to the blustery windward coast of Lāna'i. This remote wind-swept slope would be a great place to get lost. And never found. There were few signs of civilization here, not even such beginnings as lines for electricity, telephone, and cable TV. The sloping terrain, like the bleached highway, looked scorched. Stunted *kiawe* and red rock—that was it. Over the craggy landscape the wind howled.

Before long Maui and Moloka'i lay in the distance on the blue sea. Then the rusty hulk of the grounded ship came into view, listing and battered into a bare skeleton. Many years ago the Navy tried to sink the mammoth World War II liberty ship in the channel between Lāna'i and Maui. But the vessel had a mind of her own. She ran aground and all attempts to remove her failed. Today she still haunts the beach like a rotting corpse yet unburied by the sea.

Unreal. As unreal as the likelihood of our finding a sunscreen bottle on eight miles of beach presided over by this hoary wreck.

As the highway bent down to the shore and the pavement turned to sand, we found ourselves driving along the beach on a powdery path bordered by *kiawe* thickets. The wind swirled a sand contrail behind us as the Jeep got squirrelly. I shifted into four-wheel-drive.

Another mile brought a huddle of fishing shacks, erected of timbers washed ashore from capsized vessels, and the first human faces we'd seen on this desolate coast, two local fishermen mending a net. Beyond the shacks where the path ended, I did a U-turn and stopped, pointing the Jeep back toward the highway in case we needed to leave in a hurry.

"The ship is about a mile down the beach." I broke the news to Maya. "We'll have to hike."

As we stepped from the Jeep, grains of wind-blown sand bit into our bare limbs like a swarm of mosquitoes. *Gusty trades.* The tide was high and getting higher, leaving a narrow strip of beach bordered by thorny *kiawe* and littered with fishnets, ropes, Pepsi and Bud cans, driftwood, crab skeletons, rocks, and plastic containers of every color and shape. The sand literally blasted our every step as we fought our way down the inhospitable beach.

Suddenly, out of nowhere, two more Jeeps, kicking up a cloud, came flying down the sandy road.

"We've got company."

Maya glanced back, saying nothing.

The Jeeps stopped well short of ours and as I watched the sand cloud settle, two men in dark suits piled out of one and began striding slowly toward us. Another one or two remained behind in the other Jeep. *Frank O. Sun?* A good hundred yards stood between them and our own Jeep, which was beginning to look dangerously far away.

"Let's turn around."

"Turn around?" Maya arched her brows. "What about the map?"

"If we find it, Sun is going to want it too. We better head back to Lāna'i City, where there's safety in numbers."

Maya nodded and we jogged to our Jeep, hopping in before the suits came close enough to do us harm. I cranked the motor and mashed the pedal down. Sand swirled behind us, spraying tiny shrapnel on the two men as we whizzed by. I sucked in a deep breath and held it, hoping they weren't going to start waving guns. I recognized the white hair of the man who had visited my office; the other man I could only see was dark.

We flew past the Jeeps. One had a suit-and-tie now standing beside it; inside sat a man in dark glasses and hat.

When the sand settled behind us, the odd couple had shrunk to tiny stick figures in the distance running for their vehicles. Before long the two Jeeps were filling our rear-view mirrors, where they stayed all the way back to Lāna'i City.

seventeen

When I swung into the pine-lined drive to the Lodge at Koele, one of Sun's Jeeps swerved in behind us and almost spun. At remote Shipwreck Beach Maya and I were easy targets. But here at the Lodge, it would be harder to avoid witnesses.

The Lodge at Koele rambled over acres of highland woods and tropical gardens and expansive lawns. Though its patina copper roof, cozy dormer windows, and wide shaded *lānai* echoed the plantation-style architecture of the humble village below, this palace was definitely not humble. The portico over the grand entrance displayed a larger-than-life hand-painted golden pineapple, the Hawaiian symbol of hospitality.

With Sun at our backs, I was pinning my hopes on that legendary hospitality right now. Since there was no way to get back to Shipwreck Beach before nightfall without being followed, we'd best get a room.

At the reception desk a bow-tied local woman greeted us cordially, with a well-trained *"Aloha."* It was Friday in prime season—when the American heartland was buried in snow— and we had no reservation.

Predictably all standard rooms were booked.   She straightened her tie, apologized, and then explained that the Lodge was happy to offer us, instead, some of its more luxurious accommodations.   We could score a spacious "plantation" room with king-size poster bed for nearly four bills, or a two-bedroom suite for a grand. *Ho!*

"We'll take the plantation room," I said, without even glancing at Maya. I handed the receptionist my credit card and signed in: "Mr. and Mrs. Cooke." Never mind that I had no wedding ring; my companion did.

"A porter will assist you with your luggage."

"Thanks, we can manage." I pointed to Maya's small bag and then mumbled some line about preferring to travel light.

We passed through the Lodge's Southwest-inspired Great Room, an open-beamed expanse whose sunny skylights glowed on countless wingback chairs and sofas and oriental rugs, then across a wicker-chaired verandah. Out of the corner of my eye I saw two Jeeps pull under the Norfolks at the Lodge's entrance, then one man jumped from each Jeep, both as overdressed and out of place on Lāna'i as they had been on O'ahu.

"Company again." I turned to Maya, who I began to notice was rather accomplished at being unfazed.

The two men stepped into the Lodge, leaving one man inside each Jeep. Even at this distance, inside the trailing Jeep I could see the Panama hat.

"Sun seems to think we know something he doesn't," I said. "Did Corky tell him about the map?"

"No, that's why Corky was killed."

Maya said "killed" nearly as dispassionately as if she were referring to a cockroach. Now I've seen more than my share of grieving widows and lovers. And, hands down, Maya was the coolest of all. When it registered that this was the first she'd referred to Corky's death since leaving Maui, I wondered again what else this forty-six-year-old redhead wasn't talking about.

Our airy, pale blue room had enough soft angles and plush furnishings to put one in the mood for relaxation. The king-size bed, a four-poster of knotty pine, reigned over the spacious room, but left plenty of extra territory for overstuffed chairs and lounges and billowy blue curtains framing bucolic views. We had everything anybody might need: a wet bar, a safe, color TV and video player, two phones, a koa ceiling fan, and our own personal *lānai* overlooking our own personal banyan tree.

I stepped onto the teak-furnished *lānai* and watched Sun's two Jeeps, drivers only, pull into the Lodge's parking lot. Maya reclined on the four-poster bed, each post topped with a carved miniature pineapple resembling a hand grenade.

"Lovely." Maya ran her fingers over the powder-blue comforter. "Try the bed, Kai."

As she oozed admiration over our temporary lavish surroundings, I couldn't help observe, "You don't seem too broken up over your boyfriend."

"Husband," she corrected me. "Anyway, I had my cry." Fluffing a downy blue pillow, Maya turned her eyes to me. "What do we do now?"

"Wait."

"For what?" She stretched her lanky limbs on the bed like a cat.

"Darkness," I said. "In the mean time, you can make yourself comfortable."

"I will." Maya continued her feline stretching. Her copper hair glowed against the blue pillows. She made that poster bed look awfully inviting. So I made myself turn away and walk over to the desk.

Paging through the Lāna'i phone directory, I searched for the number of a surfing buddy whom I had first met years ago in the lineup at Cunahs in Waikīkī. I hadn't seen Conrad Figueira recently, and I didn't even know if Rad or his family still resided on Lāna'i. But having just one friend on this island might be a lifesaver.

I tried dialing "Angel Figueira," the first of two "Figueira" entries in the tiny book. The phone rang and rang. On the sixth ring an out of breath young woman gasped "Hello." I explained my old relationship with Conrad.

"Rad?" she said excitedly. "You're a friend of my big brother?"

Catalina told me she lived in the family home in Lāna'i City with her two children, Felipe and Maria, and their grandfather, Angel, who worked the early morning shift in the kitchen at Mānele Bay Hotel.

"Come visit us," Catalina said with warm and sincere Filipino hospitality. "Felipe and Maria would love to meet you. And Papa too. He's napping now. He goes to work every morning at five."

She gave me directions to their house on 'Ilima Avenue, and we hung up. If Maya and I ran into trouble, Catalina might just become our new best friend.

I then phoned Leimomi and left a message that I was working a case on Lāna'i and was *very* sorry to miss our date tonight. I left neither a phone number nor said at what hotel I was staying—I didn't even want to think about what kind of explaining I'd have to do if Leimomi called and Maya answered.

Maya and I stayed in the room most of the afternoon, her watching infomercials about age-defying miracle beauty cures, me sitting on the *lānai* keeping an eye on Sun's Jeeps in the parking lot. Around four, I took a walk to the sundry store and bought two penlights.

As I was leaving, I saw my albino friend in the cavernous Great Room sunk into an overstuffed leather sofa with a newspaper in front of his nose. He acted as if he didn't see me, but as I passed he peered at me over his *New York Times* and then pulled a cell phone from his shirt pocket.

When I returned to our room, Maya's impression remained in the blue comforter, but she was gone. *I knew I shouldn't have left her alone.*

Ten minutes passed. I imagined as many scenarios in which she played victim to Sun's goons as those in which she played their accomplice, compliant with their plots to an extent that did not threaten her "widow's" inheritance.

When she finally let herself in, I asked where she had been.

"Reliving beautiful memories," she explained, reclaiming her comfy spot on the poster bed.

"You and Corky stayed here?"

She nodded, her smile becoming annoyingly serene.

I walked over to the phone, definitely feeling more relaxed at the thought of Maya not being one of Sun's pawns. "I hope you liked the food then, because I'm about to make reservations for dinner. Seven?"

She nodded.

I phoned in the dinner reservation, then pulled a frosty Heineken from the wet bar and offered it to Maya.

"I don't drink," she said, recovering her voice.

I popped the cap and began to down the Heineken myself. As I was nearing the bottom, the phone rang. I let it go.

Maya looked at me as the phone rang and rang. "Aren't you going to answer it?"

"No."

I sat silently and watched Maya. She didn't move. Finally the phone stopped ringing. A message light began blinking.

I picked up the handset and played the message.

"Kai . . . ?"

Leimomi had tracked me down. And she sounded desperate.

"I did what you asked. I bought a pregnancy test kit. We need to talk. I can't bear this alone."

Pilikia. I shook my head. Trouble.

"And, Kai, why did the hotel operator say she was connecting me to the room of 'Mr. and *Mrs.* Cooke'? Who's Mrs. Cooke?"

"What's the message?" Maya was asking in my other ear.

"Wrong number." I hung up the phone.

Maya rose abruptly from the poster bed. "I'm going to take a bath in that blue tub. Do you mind?"

"Why should I mind?"

Maya said nothing more as she ambled toward the gleaming tub, leaving the door partway open behind her.

I could see her reflection in the bathroom mirror. Behind her, powder blue was the dominant hue, with soft, indirect lighting and fixtures of polished brass. Gauzy shower curtains, draped from a brass rod the size of a canon, fell into sweeping festoons with plenty of pomp and circumstance. Cream-colored throw rugs and fluffy terry towels made the scene that much more luxurious.

Maya began to undress, revealing the shapely breasts I'd been glimpsing at all day. The freckles on her face, I discovered, had cousins elsewhere. And they were sexy—each and every one. She definitely didn't look her forty-plus years. Her slender limbs were smooth and gracefully sculpted. Only around her neck could I detect the first faint lines that someday would show her age, but not yet. When she shed her panties, the triangular puff of copper hair between her legs sent shock waves through my brain.

"Join me in the bath?" Maya's voice snapped me out of my reverie. *Say what?*

Maya bent, gorgeously naked, toward the brass tub faucets and cranked on the hot. A steamy flood poured out as a war went on inside me. There was something more than a little unsavory about climbing into that steaming tub with the redhead whose "husband" had just died violently only hours before. Then there was Leimomi, whose looming pregnancy had my future hanging in the wind.

I watched as Maya sprinkled in a packet of bathing crystals. A rich, dewy, seductive scent instantly perfumed the room. *Jasmine.* I could see the hot water rising, bubbling and shimmering.

Maya swung one long bare leg over the baby blue tub rail, then the other. She slipped down into the fragrant bath. Soon only her slender neck and fiery hair showed above the rising water.

"*Ahhhh . . .*" was all she said.

I don't know how it happened exactly. It wasn't a decision I consciously made. When I slid in behind her, she remained silent. She turned and glimpsed the shark marks on my chest.

But even they didn't move her to speak. The water was almost too hot—on the edge of scalding. But before long I got used to it. I breathed in deeply and the jasmine sent filled my lungs. I cupped my hands around her breasts as she eased up onto me. Instantly she was moving and communicating, not with words, but with sighs.

We climbed higher and higher, taking each other up to an invisible summit. When we finally tumbled over it together, Maya screamed and grabbed my thighs so tightly that her nails left deep red impressions. I felt the sting, but didn't care. By then I was floating on a blue cloud.

Making love with someone I'd just met was kind of crazy. There was a sense of knowing her intimately—the warmth of her touch, the taste of her skin and hair and private places, and the exquisite feel of her love—yet I hardly knew *her* at all. Who she was, how she lived, or what she lived for.

Before the floral euphoria of the blue bath faded, there was a knock at the door. "Room Service," said a male voice.

"Did you order Room Service?" I whispered into drowsy Maya's ear.

"No, sweetie, I didn't order anything," she cooed back.

I stepped dripping from the tub, wrapped a fluffy towel around me, and headed for the door.

"Who are you looking for?" I asked through the thick wood. No reply.

I heard a tray settle to the carpet and some china and silver clinking. Then I heard footsteps—not one pair but two or three—quick footsteps making tracks down the hallway from the door.

I dialed Room Service. "Did you send a tray to our room?"

"One moment, sir . . . No, sir, Mr. Cooke. Nothing was sent to your room. Would like to order from the room service menu?"

"No, thank you. A waiter apparently left a tray by mistake at our door. You might want to send someone for it."

"Yes, sir. Immediately."

As I slipped back into Maya's warm blue world, I got to thinking. *What was on that tray?*

eighteen

Inside the dimly lighted Lodge dining room the ambiance was Old World, island-style: crystal chandeliers glinting against dark paneling of *koa* and mango; landscapes of Provence hanging beside Hawaiian quilts and a lava rock fireplace. When the *maître d'* seated us, the pearly twilight was fading to grey and I was just hashing out my plan. It wasn't an elegant plan— not so elegant as this high-toned eatery. No matter. So long as the plan worked.

Smelling fresh from her jasmine bath, Maya hardly glanced at the menu and announced, "I'm a vegetarian," then ordered portobello mushrooms with Waimānalo greens. *Whatevahs*. The four-star Pacific Rim establishment boasted fresh Island ingredients with Continental flair—Moloka'i venison carpaccio, Lāna'i mixed pheasant and quail sausage with Pinot Noir sauce, *onaga* and Kahuku mashed potatoes, and fancy wines staring at seventy clams. I went with the catch-of-the-day—fresh '*ōpakapaka*—grilled solo with no sauces, chutneys, salsas, or other fussy stuff. Just the way I like it.

If Sun were watching us dine, he kept himself hidden through the entire meal.

When the check came, it took my breath away. *Oh, well, Sun's money.* I put the meal on our hotel tab and we strolled arm-in-arm back toward our room, past illuminated orchids and lily pads and cascading bougainvillea. Beyond the lighted pathway were bubbling blue spas, and beyond the spas were darkened golf links and hills and woods. Suddenly sensing someone behind us, I stopped under a torrent of bougainvillea and drew Maya to me. I whispered, "Let's put on a show."

Maya kissed me as her roving grey-green eyes glanced over my shoulder and found one of the bubbling spas. "Want to make love in the spa?"

"Later."

Her slender fingers ran down the buttons of my aloha shirt, past swaying palms and *hula* dancers.

"Later," I said again, though she was getting good at distracting me. "Listen, if Sun's man drops back, we can slip into the darkness and then run to the golf clubhouse. Up there on the rise." I pointed. "Follow the cart path and stay behind the trees so no one can see you."

"You're no fun." Maya pinched my behind.

"Have you forgotten why we're here?" I reached into my khakis and pulled out one of the two penlights. "Take this. But don't turn it on, if you can avoid it."

Behind us, our tail lit a cigarette and slowly edged away. Since we'd been at the Lodge, Sun's men had appeared to be working in solo shifts, perhaps hoping not to arouse suspicion about their un-resort-like attire and conduct.

"Let's move," I whispered. We split off and jogged through the maze of gardens and up the cart path toward the first fairway.

Behind the clubhouse we finally met up, both of us puffing. When the blood stopped pounding in my ears, I listened to reassure myself we hadn't been followed and then, clasping her warm hand, led Maya quietly into the dark woods.

Snapping on our penlights, we huffed up a foothill trail through a grove of ironwoods and pines. In less than half mile of meandering, the trail intersected the road to Shipwreck Beach.

Six miles stood between the Lodge at Koele and Shipwreck Beach. *Six miles.* Sun would be watching our Jeep, so that was out. But it was a nice evening for a hike. The air was cool, even a bit chilly at this elevation, and luckily the blustery trades had died down.

We stepped along the sloping highway, alone under the stars. Any approaching vehicle would give us plenty of warning to conceal ourselves, for headlights and a motor's hum would carry a long way in this silent night. The terrain looked less desolate by night than by day, a dark country road winding down an endless grade. We could have been in any rural spot, except for the lights of Lahaina flickering across the channel.

The moon soon rose above the sea, painting Maui's distant twin mounds pale amber. The highway took on an eerie glow. I hoped Maya would complain of sore feet—so I could too. But she kept on, her hips swaying rhythmically in front of me.

I glanced behind us, looking for two pairs of Jeep headlights. I glanced behind us again and again. No sign of Mr. Sun.

It was past midnight when we finally reached Shipwreck Beach. A low tide offered more sand for our throbbing feet to tread on than the narrow strip of the morning. Bleached remnants of sea creatures scattered about glowed like ghouls in the moonlight.

Our every stride brought more cans, containers, and debris to sift through—Miller Genuine Draft, Kikkoman soy sauce, a lonely flipper, Tide detergent, a rusty fire extinguisher, frayed rope—in search of our sunscreen bottle.

"What kind of sunscreen are we looking for?"

"Coppertone," Maya said. "Bronze bottle. Number 8." She paused. "Oh, yeah, Corky said to look by a rusty freight container washed ashore near the stranded ship."

She tells me this now? Could she really be that much of an airhead? I stepped gingerly among the debris. *Or was this a wild goose chase after all, with Maya in the lead?*

As we hiked the beach toward the wrecked ship, behind us I spotted two flashlights, about a quarter mile back, combing the sand like search beacons. They could have belonged to fishermen, but I doubted it.

"Guess who?" I pointed to the roving lights.

Maya didn't even hear me. Her mouth had dropped open.

Before us loomed the moonlit ship, its rotting, ghostlike corpse still unburied by the sea. Heavy swells were battering it and exploding like skyrockets in the moon's glow. I got chicken-skin.

Opposite the distant ship sat the freight container on the beach, sprayed by the shore break. The rust-orange container had apparently plunged from a freighter, spilled its cargo, and washed ashore. One of its two doors had been ripped off and lay twenty yards away in the sand.

I glanced down the dark beach. The roving beams kept coming. Now human figures crossed in front of the beams, picking their way through the debris as they walked. "Where's the map?" I asked again.

Maya shone her penlight inside the rusty freight container. Crabs with big menacing claws scuttled every which way through the dark and shallow sloshing seawater. Their powerful pincers and beady eyes seemed to threaten intruders: "Don't even think about it setting foot in here!" Only those twin searchlights closing in on us could possibly prompt me into that container.

No need. Maya evidently knew right where to look. Under the lip of the doorsill—high above the crabs and sheltered from wind and sea, there it was: a bronze bottle. Coppertone 8.

nineteen

"Unscrew the cap."

Maya's eyes met mine, and something in them glinted like a devious child's. She twisted off the cap.

I shone my penlight on a rolled piece of paper inside the neck of the bottle. It looked dry and clean. A pencil or car key or small finger could, with patience, fish it out.

"That's Corky's map." Maya peered at the rolled paper and smiled strangely.

"Screw on the cap and let's go."

"Go? Don't you want to see it?"

I pointed down the beach at the wandering beams. "Let's move."

"Where?"

"Hiking trails head *mauka* every mile or so along the beach. They're full of *kiawe* thickets and out of our way, but they may be our *only* way."

Maya nodded and we took off down the beach, away from the lights.

About a mile beyond the wrecked ship, we came to a sandy trail twisting up several miles toward Lāna'i City. It didn't make sense to go back to the room now, where Sun's men would be waiting for us. It'd be better to push ahead and try to get off this island. It was now two a.m. We had miles to go before dawn. And the twin beams kept coming.

We took the *mauka* trail.

Hours later, in the distance, we saw a faint flickering. Lānaʻi City. The moon in the west was setting over the tranquil sea, while the eastern sky behind us was turning the color of a blushing peach.

No more roving beams. No head lamps. Had we shaken them?

The twinkling village stretched out before us in a luminous grid. Cottage windows of early risers glowed pale yellow against the brighter checkerboard of streetlights. We headed for one of those cottages, the home of Angel Figuiera.

Tin-roofed plantation dwellings with postage stamp-sized lawns lined ʻIlima Avenue in colors that, even under glaring street lights, looked wild: lemon yellow, cinnamon red, cornflower blue. Evidence of family life abounded: boogie boards, bicycles with training wheels, barbecues, toy Jeeps, Igloo coolers. A puppy whined. A lone rooster crowed. Hard to believe that among this reassuring domesticity a drug lord might be lurking.

Most cottages didn't have legible numbers, but from the few that did, we seemed to be moving in the right direction. There it was—537 affixed to a lavender cottage with a rust-freckled GMC truck occupying the lawn.

Five in the morning is a strange time to knock at someone's door. We had little choice.

A short, wiry old man appeared in a white chef's apron that contrasted his wrinkled, raisin brown skin. He must have lived seventy years, maybe more, under the tropic sun. Despite his weathered appearance, Angel Figuiera's lively eyes sparkled like an excited boy's.

"Mr. Figuiera? I'm a friend of Rad's from Oʻahu—Kai Cooke."

"Eh, Kai, Catalina bin tol' me you call." Out came his sunny smile and his pidgin.

"Sorry we come so early." I shifted to pidgin myself. "Dis my frien' Maya. We get some kine *pilikia*. Can help us out, or what?"

"Shoots . . ." The old man smiled.

"We need catch da firs' boat to Lahaina from Mānele Bay dis morning, so dat"—I hesitated—"so dat nobody see us."

"No need explain. You n' Maya come wit' me to Mānele Bay Hotel. I work dere."

"You go to work soon?"

"Yeah, right now in da truck." He waved toward the GMC. "Climb in da back, in da shell. Nobody see you in dere."

I was grateful for local-style hospitality. No need to explain motive, however bizarre, even shady. After our nightlong hike, I had little energy to spin a yarn about what we'd been through, or what we might face ahead. Sometimes mysteries are best left that way.

Angel's pickup rattled through the few blocks of Lānaʻi City, then turned down Highway 44, the two lane blacktop also known as Mānele Road that ran about five unswerving miles, then began to weave as it approached the cliffs of Mānele Bay.

"Da boat to Maui no leave 'til eight in da morning," Angel said through the sliding window between the cab and the shell.

"Dat's OK," I said.

"Da harbor jus' one short walk from Mānele Bay," Angel explained. "You like come to da hotel?"

"You sure no problem?" I asked.

"Nah, I take you t'rough da kitchen. I'm one *preparation chef*." Angel said in formal English, pronouncing each syllable of his title carefully. "I prepare da pineapples and papaya and mango fo' da guests' breakfas'—lunch too. I experience' wit' pineapple," Angel laughed. "T'irty years in da pineapple fields—I pick 'em. Now in da resort, I slice 'em. I da 'pineapple man.'"

As Angel approached the cliffs, Maya gazed longingly at Mānele Bay, dead ahead in the gauzy twilight.

"Over dere, dat's da resort where I work now," Angel said. "Job mo' easier, mo' bettah pay. Go figgah."

The Manele Bay Hotel spread its meandering Mediterranean-tiled wings around the sheltered bay where dolphins are known to play and *malahinis* bake in the tropic sun. Unlike the cool Lodge at Koele, this oceanfront resort embraced the typically sun-splashed beach.

But there wasn't much sun at quarter past five, just a pink glow heightening in the east. Nearly three hours to cool our heels. The more time we gave Sun to find us, the more chance he would. But what was the likelihood of Frank O. Sun thinking to look for us in a resort kitchen? Zilch, I hoped.

Angel punched in at 5:28 a.m., then we followed him through a maze of hallways to the huge kitchen, where he donned a chef's cap embroidered with the resort's name in royal blue. At stainless preparation tables *sous chefs* were already at work slicing tangy tropic fruits for the breakfast buffet: kiwi, mango, pineapple, papaya—while mingled whiffs of cinnamon, coconut, and buttery oats suggested that the pastry chefs had started work even earlier.

My stomach growled. I saw Maya eyeing a tray of fragrant muffins. Since we had just hiked through the night without food, I suspected she was as ravenous as I. Angel must have seen the look of hunger in our eyes.

"Dis way," he smiled warmly. "Da employees' dining room."

Angel led us a short distance from the kitchen to a room where resort workers were eating a very early breakfast. A smaller sampling of the hotel's guest fare was laid out in a buffet line.

"OK wit' da boss if we eat?" I wondered out loud.

"He don' min'," Angel winked. "He don' know and he don' min'. Or he put 'em on my tab, no worry."

Maya and I filed through the buffet line heaping on fruits of every variety, elegant pastries, and, for me, scrambled eggs and breakfast meats. We filled our plates, then dug in, as if only hours earlier I hadn't forked over two bills for dinner at the Lodge's swanky restaurant.

After breakfast Maya found an unnoticed corner of the employees' lounge to snooze in, and I kept watch on a secluded terrace overlooking the bright blue bay. To ensure we didn't miss our ferry, I set my alarm watch for seven thirty. Even if I had dared to, I was too wired to sleep. I kept turning over our options for escape once we reached Maui. None of them perfect.

When I stepped back into the employees' lounge to wake Maya, she was gone. As my watch ticked toward eight I wondered if she and the sunscreen bottle had flown. I tried not to worry. Her disappearances were becoming routine.

A few minutes later she casually strolled into the lounge.

"Where have you been?" I asked the obvious with all the enthusiasm of a soldier after a twelve-mile forced march.

"Reliving beautiful memories of Mānele Bay," she replied. "Corky and I—"

"Do you still have the map?"

"Why wouldn't I?" She opened her purse and fished out the bronze sunscreen bottle.

"OK, let's go." I led her to the employees' dressing rooms where—with the blessing of Angel, if not his boss—we changed into a couple of unattended wait-staff uniforms: royal blue aloha shirts, slacks, and embossed baseball caps. Maya slipped the sunscreen bottle into the pocket of her aloha shirt, where the staff customarily kept their order pads and pens, then twined up her long hair under the blue cap. I practiced slouching in my new outfit, so I might be taken for a tired waiter on whom onlookers would spare no more than a casual glance. With my sore feet, working up a shuffling gait was no problem.

We tracked down Angel again, thanked him for the food and clothes, and asked about getting a ride to the ferry.

"No worry," he said, smiling his *aloha* smile. He led us up a spiral staircase to the resort's marble-columned entrance. From there a van whisked us to Mānele Harbor like two hotel workers heading for a weekend getaway on Maui.

The Lahaina-Lāna'i ferry idled into the harbor as we arrived. About the size of a city bus, the boldly red-white-and-blue-striped vessel floated high in the water and had two decks spacious enough to accommodate more than the few passengers waiting with us to board. The lower deck was enclosed by dark glass; the upper, behind the wheelhouse, was open to the morning sun. At the stern, four gaping pipes rumbled with the throaty authority of twin diesels.

This appeared to be no "chug-chug" ferry, but one that could get up and move. The twenty-five mile trip between Lāna'i and Lahaina was scheduled to take only forty minutes. The fast clip would suit me just fine. The sooner we got away from the Pineapple Isle, the better.

The ferry docked and the engines shut down. I scanned the other passengers who boarded with us. None of them looked the type to run drugs. Maya and I took comfy velour seats on the lower deck. Soft fusion jazz—Kenny G's mellow sax— wafted through the air-conditioned cabin. I thought of Tommy. The pseudo-soothing ambiance inside the ferry was at odds with the increasing tension I felt every minute we remained docked. I looked up into the wheelhouse, where the captain's digital clock said 7:58. I took a deep breath.

One minute later the twin diesels started up with a roar, then settled into syncopated hum. The steward removed the boarding plank. Maya put her head on my shoulder. "It's almost like being on vacation," she said.

"Almost," I replied. She sure was taking this mad dash for our lives in stride.

I scanned tiny harbor, a lava rock breakwater sheltering a half dozen sailboats and small fishing vessels, but saw no evidence of Frank O. Sun or his well-dressed lieutenants. Not on the breakwater. Not on any nearby boat.

Then up on the distant rise, I caught sight of a Jeep weaving down toward us in a hurry. No, two Jeeps. Moving fast.

Maya looked up then and clutched the sunscreen bottle in the pocket of her aloha shirt. As the ferry chugged toward the harbor's mouth, the two Jeeps stormed into the parking lot. A man in dark glasses and suit jumped from one of the Jeeps and waved his arms. He shouted something at the boat. I couldn't hear his words over the throbbing motors.

"Captain," the steward shouted up to the wheelhouse, "More passengers?"

I looked at Maya. She looked at me. Neither of us said a word.

twenty

The steward shouted again. "Take the passengers aboard?"

The cabin clock read 8:01. The captain cranked the wheel toward the open sea and revved the twin diesels. In a cloud of salt spray and billowing exhaust, the ferry roared from Mānele Harbor.

As we began climbing swells outside the breakwater, the two Jeeps became mere specks behind us. Soon the ferry swung around the rocky southern tip of Lāna'i and into the channel to West Maui. Lahaina was not yet visible, only the green cane fields scaling the mountain behind it. The drone of the diesels, the bow rising and falling over the swells, and my lack of sleep would normally have made me doze off. But not today. My mind was racing.

Before we hit Maui we needed a plan. *How to get back to O'ahu?*

We could try to evade Sun by boarding a flight from Kahului to Kaua'i or Moloka'i or the Big Island, then connecting to O'ahu. Wandering Kahului Airport, however, could be risky. Or we could drive to remote, tiny Hāna Airport in East Maui where Sun surely wouldn't go. But the trip would set us back half a day. Our best bet was to try the commuter airport at Kapalua—just up the road from Lahaina. Island Hopper flew Twin Otters from Kapalua almost hourly. Even if Sun pursued us there, we would most likely take off before he arrived.

As the ferry cruised across the channel, we were surrounded by islands: Lāna'i fading behind us, brooding Kaho'olawe on our right, cliffy Moloka'i on our left, and cloud-wreathed Maui dead ahead.

Maya was missing this awesome array of islands. The twin diesels' rhythmic hum had put her to slack-mouthed sleep. I heard a clack on the floor under her seat, then spotted an object near her feet the size of a cigarette pack. I plucked it off the deck. *A cell phone.* There was a call-back number on the screen, but no messages. I watched Maya's even breathing as I tried to memorize the number before returning the phone to the floor. Then I peeked into the pocket of her aloha shirt. The bronze sunscreen bottle was still there.

The crossing from Lāna'i to Maui took every one of the scheduled forty minutes. But before long the engines quieted down again to a syncopated idle. Ahead, Lahaina Harbor's antique lighthouse pointed skyward like an ivory needle. Coconut palms and spreading banyans stood sentinel over the old whaling port, with its vintage square-rigged ships and legendary Pioneer Inn. I'd never been so glad to see the red roof of that storied old inn—a place where whalers once imbibed their grog, and whale watchers still do today.

At nine on Saturday morning in prime whale-watching season, Lahaina Harbor was jumping. Sunburned *malahini* lined the decks of dozens of vessels, powered and sail, that ply the sea in search of those leviathans. Near the harbor's entrance, surfers rode lazy little rollers. I envied those board riders, *surfing free.*

As the ferry docked I scanned countless cabs and vans and passenger cars flanking the Pioneer Inn, and on bordering Wharf and Hotel Streets. I focused momentarily on each vehicle, looking for telltale signs of Frank O. Sun. Though I saw none, I wasn't fully reassured.

Maya and I disembarked and lost ourselves in the after-breakfast crowd on Front Street. Lahaina town was as lively as its harbor. The main drag bustled with tourists eyeing I Got Lei'd on Maui T-shirts, Cheeseburger in Paradise, time-share condo deals, you name it. On Front Street we boarded the Lahaina Trolley, which runs north to the resorts of Kāʻanapali, and blended in with the rest of the aloha shirts and bikinis on their way to work or play.

The trolley, a mock cable car, breezed through town, then along the coast a few miles to Whaler's Village at Kāʻanapali. From there we caught a shuttle up slope to tiny Kapalua Airport. On the tarmac stood a Twin-Otter, my old friend: eighteen seats, two propellers, the boxy shape of a mini-van. Small, but enough airplane to fly us back to Oʻahu.

Minutes later, the Twin-Otter lifted off over the golden sands and pale jade reefs of Kāʻanapali's famous beach, then the deep blue channel between Maui and the shadowy cliffs of Molokaʻi.

"Open the sunscreen bottle," I shouted into Maya's ear above the engine roar.

"Here . . . on the airplane?" she yelled back.

We were seated at the rear of the Twin-Otter—the last row by the door—enduring a ear-shattering din. The turboprops screamed, the cabin vibrated, the whole airplane audibly throbbed.

"Nobody's looking," I yelled. I had already reassured myself that no one aboard appeared to be employed by Sun, and no one was manifesting much interest in how two resort workers were spending their Saturday off.

Maya scanned the passengers, then she unscrewed the cap. She stuck her little finger in the tiny bottle neck and coaxed out the rolled paper.

"It's not a map," she said, even before unrolling the small sheet. "It's directions."

I suspected she had already peeked.

The document was handwritten in blue-black ink on buff stationary imprinted "The Lodge at Koele," where Maya and Corky had apparently spent a lost weekend. At the end was a little crude drawing of what looked like a church steeple. Corky had damn lousy penmanship. Or he must have scribbled this thing in a big hurry. It read:

Hey, Babe,

Drive to Waimea Bay. Look for the bell tower at the mission on the n– side of the bay. The stuff is in the tower. Go there when the church is open for mass on Sunday so you can climb the tower. At the top is a bench under the windows where you can s– the whole bay. Look under the bench seat.

If you read this, it means I'm gone. Sorry I didn't make it with you, Babe. But this map is your insurance policy.

Luv ya,

Corky

"Is it what you expected?" I yelled into Maya's ear over the roar.

"Yes and no," she said. "Corky took me to Mass once at that church. It was strange because he wasn't religious. He was *spiritual*—but not conventionally religious. It all makes sense now."

"Sunday may be our best bet to climb the bell tower. But we'll go have a look today anyway. Most Catholic churches hold a mass or two on Saturday evening."

After the Twin Otter touched down in Honolulu, we headed for the car rental agencies—no way could we stroll up to my Impala in the lot without being spotted. As I waited at the Hertz counter, craning my neck to spot any dark suits lurking, I called my office for messages. Off Oʻahu now for nearly twenty-four hours, I wondered if Summer had checked in.

The first message was from Leimomi—she needed me. I had forgotten to return her last call. I felt terrible, but it would have to wait longer still.

There were three other messages.

"Mr. Kai Cooke? Your Jeep is overdue." The Lānaʻi Plantation Store. I wondered how much not returning that Jeep was going to cost me. Or Sun.

The next message was from attorney Grossvendt. "Any news about my BMW convertible . . . ?"

I had news: He would never see his beloved BMW again, unless Sun got busted and all his assets were seized. If so, the car would probably come back in pieces.

The last message was in a low and heavily accented voice: "Mr. Cooke, I think you make some fatal mistake. I say 'Investigation over.' And I mean *over.*"

Frank O. Sun. I envisioned his dark glasses and Panama hat.

"You are paid handsomely. Is this not true? I give you one last chance . . . like a gentleman, yes? A word to the wise: consider most carefully."

I heard a click. No message from Summer.

Maya and I piled into a Hertz Ford and drove to Waimea Bay. We didn't talk much. Just as well. I was thinking about Summer and wondering whether my beating Sun to the ice would help her, or hurt her. I hoped the former. But it was now out of my control.

As we pulled onto the H-1 ramp, I checked the rear view mirrors. If Sun knew we had the only map to his missing treasure, he wouldn't let us out of his sight for long. He had to be back there somewhere.

When we got to the bay, Kamehameha Highway surrounding it was choked with traffic. I braked and we were stopped momentarily on the ridge. The air was pregnant with mist. Spectators, two and three and four deep, lined the road gawking at the drama below.

Waimea was breaking!

The whole crew was out. Big wave legends and newcomers and wannabes. A dozen surfers on stiletto-like big guns stroked for each massive swell. The sets looked good. Probably eighteen to twenty feet.

Nearly every surfer on earth knows the view from this ridge. The classic scene is portrayed often in the surf media—the horseshoe-shaped bay, the mountainous waves, and their daring riders. And in the background, always, rises the mission's bell tower, higher than the highest winter waves.

That surfer Corky McDahl had chosen this tower in which to hide his treasure, his deliverance, his salvation, made perfect sense. As it loomed into view, the huge monolith took on new meaning for me: the end of the line for this twisted and deadly treasure hunt.

We crawled in the traffic, a solid line of cars and vans and trucks wrapping around the bay. Finally passing the beach park entrance, where police were turning vehicles away, we crossed Waimea stream and curved around the bay's north side.

The gravel lot in front of the mission looked deserted. *No Saturday Mass?* I got out and stepped to the church. It was locked up tight. The front doors were bolted, as were the side entrances. And the bell tower.

I walked around the building until I found a sign: Mass Every Sunday—7:30 and 9:30 a.m.

Corky had been right. Our treasure hunt would have to wait until tomorrow.

twenty-one

We followed Kamehameha Highway north past ʻEhukai and Sunset. Both breaks, like Waimea, were cranking and the highway and beaches packed.

At Kahuku Point, the highway bent east and then south to Lāʻie, where a narrow side road marked by a single sign led *makai* to the Mālaekahana Bay campgrounds. We turned in. Mālaekahana's tranquil beachside campsites in February lay mostly empty, unlike in spring and summer when tents sprout like wild mushrooms. Technically, a state permit is required to camp at Mālaekahana, which means driving downtown to Punchbowl Street. We had no time for that.

"Do you like sleeping on the sand?" I asked Maya.

She knit her brows. Surprisingly, the footloose redhead didn't appear to relish the idea. She didn't even suggest sex on the beach.

"It's not exactly the Lodge at Koele," I said, "but at least there are cold showers and Sun shouldn't look for us here."

Strong trades bent the ironwoods along the shore as we stepped from the car onto a bed of their pine-like needles, within a stone's throw of the rumbling surf. It was wild out there. Wet and wild.

I borrowed Maya's cell and called Tommy Woo. But before punching in his number, I left her at the campsite and hiked to the restrooms. I didn't want her to hear the details of my dealings with Sun.

After Tommy told his obligatory first joke, I gave him Sun's telephone number and asked Tommy to call him. I wanted to contact Sun personally, but not reveal our location or that I was calling from Maya's phone.

"Block your caller ID," I added.

"It's always blocked," Tommy said. "Let's keep it simple. You talk and I'll record your voice and play it back for Sun."

"OK." I took a breath. "Here goes . . . ."

"Recording," Tommy said.

Frank O. Sun, listen up: Harm Summer McDahl and you will never see your ice again. I'm not talking more until you let Summer go . . ."

I thanked Tommy, then left a voice mail for Detective Brian Tong at Narco-Vice, telling him succinctly what I had learned about Sun and his organization. If I didn't make it through the day tomorrow, at least the authorities would profit from my investigation. I then hiked back to the campsite where Maya was gazing out to sea, as if searching for a lost and lonely speck in the boiling surf.

For the rest of the night we lay low. Night comes quickly to the tropics in winter. After sunset, twilight briefly appears, then vanishes. Suddenly we were in the dark.

I set my watch alarm for 6:00 a.m. and we slept under the stars, not on the beach, but on ironwood needles. The needles might as well have been cast from iron, for all the sleep I got.

Maya made no overtures that night. She even stopped asking for my birth sign. Her game was over, I guessed. Or maybe last night's hike had just taken the starch out of both of us.

When my alarm rang Sunday morning, a razor-thin orange line glowed above the turbulent sea. By six-thirty we were heading north on Kamehameha Highway.

The surf was still up. Following a pickup truck with a half dozen boards piled in back, we stopped just short of Waimea Bay and pulled into the mission. The car behind us also turned in. Then another. Early arrivers to seven-thirty Mass.

The mission's doors, unlike yesterday, were wide open. We followed in a young couple and their ponytailed *keiki* who walked down the center aisle, stopped by a pew, genuflected, stepped in, and turned down the kneeling bench to pray. The mission was as small as the typical side-chapel of a larger church, and was overshadowed by the massive bell tower behind it. The pews were polished dark mahogany with kneeling benches upholstered in red vinyl. Overhead, ceiling fans whirred. It was cool and quiet inside, except for the shuffling of parishioners' feet and the crack of the wooden benches being turned down against the floor.

"Find us a seat," I said to Maya as I stepped toward the rear foyer. "I'm going to look around."

When I glanced up from the foyer's skylight at that huge tower looming overhead like a medieval fortress, I couldn't help thinking: *The view of the bay from up there must be awesome.*

One thing was clear: to climb to the top I would first have to break in through a solid wood door with an old fashioned keyhole lock, the kind you find these days only in antique chests and steamer trunks. A lock like that can usually be picked, but it would have to be picked quietly.

I rejoined Maya in the chapel just as the priest rose in a long white robe, spread his arms wide like a cliff diver, and uttered in a deep, resonant voice:

"In the name of the Father, and the Son, and the Holy Spirit . . ."

"Amen," the rising parishioners responded in unison. I said "Amen" too, hoping for divine intervention to guide me up that tower.

I looked around us. The mostly local crowd filled the little church to the brim: babies in mothers' arms, toddlers, teens, *tūtū*, uncles, cousins. It was a family affair and the feeling was good. Behind the priest a vaulted arch was inscribed God Is Love. And through open windows framing the bright blue bay I could hear the thunder of surf. *Big* surf.

"The grace of our Lord Jesus Christ . . . be with you all," intoned the priest.

"And also with you," the parishioners responded.

On each pillar between the church's open windows hung a bas-relief depicting one of the fourteen stations of the cross—Via Dolorosa, the way of suffering—seven stations on either side of the chapel. White marble statues of Mary and Joseph stood behind us, each adorned with a green *haku lei*. Not the kind of scene for Sun in his Panama and shades.

"The grace and peace of God our Father . . . be with you," the priest continued.

"And also with you . . ." the parishioners replied.

Then the tuneful choir, a dozen strong, began singing their hearts out. I mumbled along. The Hawaiian *wahine* leading the choir broke into a solo, while strumming a guitar and directing three *keiki* playing ʻukulele. Soon everybody was singing merrily. Me, I kept mumbling and watching and waiting.

Maya and I did our best to rise and kneel and pray with the faithful. Though we were always off a beat. Personally, I could have used some soul cleansing right then, but I had work to do.

When the priest took up the sacred host, the chalice and the wafers for Holy Communion, I prepared to make my move. The priest raised the chalice and solemnly crossed himself, then the choir sang like earth-bound angels, *"Al-le-lu-ia! Al-le-lu-ia!"* Parishioners rose one pew at a time and filed forward to take Communion. I tapped Maya on the shoulder. "Wait for me at the car after Mass."

Maya stepped toward the altar with the others. I slipped to the back of the church, then into the foyer adjoining the bell tower.

Danger—No Admittance said a sign on the dark lacquered door leading to the tower. With only my keys and a tiny keychain jackknife so small it passes airport security, I worked the lock, while the Communion hymns covered the clinks and clanks of my lock picking. First I tried my keys: Apartment key. Office key. I wiggled each key inside the keyhole. I even tried the rental car key. No luck. Suddenly the choir's sweet *"Al-le-lu-ia!"* ceased and the priest said: "The Lord be with you . . ."

I didn't have much time. Then I tried my Impala's key— old-style, long and skinny. I heard a promising *click* . . . but then that was all. The tiny jackknife was my last hope. I opened the longer blade, slowly inserted it, and moved inside the lock.

Another promising *click* . . . followed by a louder *click* . . . *click*. *Yes!* Finally, the lock sprung.

The bell tower door opened to mustiness and semi-darkness. Rusty folding chairs and card tables layered with dust leaned against two walls. In the center, a spiral of wooden stairs. I mounted the creaky wood that serpentined up into the shadows. Through the viewing ports above came a brilliant light. With each creaking step, I rose toward it.

The choir cranked up again, guitars and 'ukulele and off-key voices:

> *Kindness and truth shall meet;*
> *Justice and peace shall kiss . . .*

The choir's voices grew fainter as I climbed, their fading hymn soon blending with another. The hymn of booming surf.

When I finally reached the tower's summit, I saw a bench lining each wall of the empty belfry, just as Corky had said. The benches doubled as storage bins; each could be lifted to reveal an enclosed compartment. In one of these compartments would be the prize. One million worth of methamphetamine ice.

As I moved toward one wall, I couldn't help but gaze out the viewing port. The bay was cranking! Swell after swell steaming in. And plenty surfers taking the big drop.

I tore my eyes away and considered the bench compartments. There were four—four chances.

I tried the bench opposite Waimea first, facing down the coast toward Pipeline and Sunset. Prying the seat up with my fingers produced cobwebs and a coil of rope. That was it.

Next I tried the bench facing *mauka* toward the sacrificial *heiau* and Waimea Stream. Empty.

I tried the one facing out to the open sea, where those huge rollers swept around the point into the Bay. More junk: a stack of yellowed copies of the *Daily Missal,* a mousetrap with a decapitated mouse, a cheap screw cap bottle of wine, a used condom.

That left the last bench facing Waimea Bay, where Corky had started this whole mess. I should have guessed. It made perfect sense.

Slowly I pried up the bench seat. My eyes scoured the empty space.

twenty-two

Nothing.

Or was there something? I noticed some sparkling dust and reached down and with my fingertips, extracting a gleaming speck. It was almost crystal-clear, like rock candy.

The ice had been here and now it was gone. *How could Sun have found it before we did?* We had the only map, according to Maya. Had Corky, before he died, revealed the location to the drug lord? If so, why was Sun still following us?

"It's gone," I told Maya in the mission's gravel lot.

Her face went blank. "It can't be," she said.

"This is all that's left." I held in my palm the little crystal of ice. "Somebody got here first."

"They lied to me." The words spilled out as if Maya were alone. Her eyes darkened to the impenetrable jade of a Waimea wave.

"Who lied?"

"The men who took Corky."

"*Took* Corky? You said they *killed* Corky. Remember his slipper and sunglasses, his spilled blood?"

"They told me to say that"—she looked away from me—"to tell you, so you'd think I was the only one left who knew where the ice was." She ran her fingers through her hair. "And they did kill a man, right in front of me. But not Corky."

I didn't know whether to believe anything this woman said anymore. I started up the car.

"It was the guy who hired Corky—Damon DiCarlo." She sounded pleading now. "They told me if I didn't lead them to the ice, the same thing would happen to Corky."

"Then why didn't they take both of you?" I turned off the engine and looked hard at her. "Why leave you behind?"

"Corky wouldn't tell them where the ice was. And he convinced them I knew nothing. But they thought *you* did and told me to go with you. Once we found the ice, they said they'd release Corky and pay me ten thousand dollars."

"And you believed that?"

She shrugged. "I had to."

"So all along you've been cooperating with Sun?" Her seduction routine suddenly made sense—it wasn't my irresistible attraction, but my usefulness in retrieving her boyfriend.

"What else could I do?"

"Think, Maya. You're not getting anything from Sun, probably not even your boyfriend."

"I'll see Corky again," she said defiantly.

"Did you call Sun and tell him where the ice was hidden?"

"*No!*"

"Can the lies, Maya."

"Mr. Sun gave me a phone number, but I didn't call. *Honest.*"

"You mean, you didn't call since Lāna'i. That's why you kept disappearing, isn't it?"

"Yes, but it was before we found the map. I haven't talked with Mr. Sun since. I swear. That's why he kept following us."

"If you didn't tell Sun, he obviously got it out of Corky. And if Corky was alive, he's not anymore. Your boyfriend double-crossed the organization—look what Sun did to DiCarlo."

"I want to go back to Maui," Maya said abruptly. "Corky will meet me there."

"Let me see your cell phone and then I'll drive you to the airport."

She looked befuddled, but reached into her pants pocket and handed me her tiny Motorola. I checked her call log for Sun's number and dialed.

On the first ring a heavy voice said "Sun."

"Mr. Frank O. Sun?"

"Yes. Who is speaking?"

"Kai Cooke."

"Ah, Mr. Cooke. You follow still errant ways? You forget investigation over, do you?"

"Mr. Sun, you've got your ice—thanks to me. If I hadn't found Corky, you'd be nowhere—like you were before I took this case."

"Beware of pride, Mr. Cooke. An emotion most unwholesome."

"My message is simple . . ." I paused for effect. "Let my client go. Narco-Vice would love to hear all I know about your organization. If you hurt Summer, I'm on the phone. Think about it." Sun didn't need to know I had already called Narco-Vice.

"You forget the husband, Mr. Cooke."

"I didn't forget. I just don't believe Corky McDahl is alive." I watched Maya flinch. "Good-bye, Mr. Sun."

I hung up.

Maya bristled. "You didn't have to say that about Corky."

"Not to be cruel, Maya, but if your boyfriend is still walking this earth, I'd be very surprised. You can call Sun and speak to him yourself, if you like." I handed back her cell phone.

She was quiet for a moment. Then she said, "I want to go home to Maui."

Minutes later we were cruising by Hale'iwa, then pineapple fields, coffee groves and Schofield Barracks. Finally we caught the freeway to the airport.

I dropped Maya at the inter-island terminal. I wasn't worried about her. She knew how to take care of herself.

"Sorry to have to ask you this, Kai," she said stepping from the rental car. "I need airfare."

"You need what?" I couldn't believe my ears.

"Airfare to Maui." She shook her copper hair, which in the full sun seemed to burst into flame.

More than anything I wanted to be rid of this woman. I reached into my wallet. From the wad of hundreds Summer had given me that fateful morning at Denny's, one was left. One green Ben Franklin—the *only* bill in my wallet. I gave it to her.

"Bon voyage."

She grinned and then kissed me passionately. I admit I didn't stop her. With her arms tight around me, her breasts pressed against me, I recalled that jasmine-scented blue bathtub at the Lodge at Koele. When she broke off the kiss, she announced: "You're warm-hearted and generous. You must be a Leo." Maya nodded. "Yes, I bet you're a Leo."

Still smiling, Maya glided into the terminal. She had lied to me for most of the forty-eight hour blur we were together.

And I felt guilty that I had given into her seductions. I also felt oddly sad upon seeing her go. I watched as she stepped gracefully into the terminal, then broke into a run. Was she running to or running from?

Whatevahs. Maya was gone.

When I returned the rental car at the airport, it seemed as if we'd had it for days. I put the charge on a credit card, then walked to the parking garage to retrieve my Impala. I had no idea what Sun might have done with my classic Chevy. But the teal Impala was still there, looking a little dusty but unharmed. I peeked under the car for explosive devices. *Nah, they wouldn't waste the powder on me.*

It started up on the first try; I swung in line to pay for parking and suddenly realized my wallet was empty. The bill for parking nearly three days would be at least thirty dollars.

When my turn at the window came I pulled in front of the attendant, a woman in a flowered muʻumuʻu the size of a tent. "I was just dropping off a friend at the terminal," I said. "I got in the wrong lane."

"Ticket?" she asked.

"Don't have one. I must have left it at the lot entrance."

A cloud crossed the attendant's face. She scanned the thin layer of dust on my Impala's hood. Obviously the car had sat several days in the garage. "Got to talk to one supahvisah."

"I'm really in a hurry," I pleaded. "It wasn't my fault. I mean it was, but I won't do it again."

"Auwe!" She let out an exasperated breath. Horns blew. The line of cars behind me was growing.

"I return da favah someday, yeah?" I hauled out my pidgin, winked, and hoped for the best.

She gave me serious stink eye, then suddenly the gate went up.

"Tanks, eh?" I drove away.

Maunakea Street never looked better. I was glad to be home. I walked through the flower shop, saying hello to Mrs. Fujiyama, who peered at me sourly over her glasses. I glanced to the rear of the shop where were Chastity was working, and Joon and Blossom. No Leimomi.

"Upstairs . . ." Mrs. Fujiyama said without apparent reference to anything. Did she mean Leimomi?

I climbed the orange shag and marched past Madame Zenobia's. The psychic shop was shut tight. Ahead I could see the full-color surfer on my door and, yes, someone was waiting, sitting on the floor, hunched over as if in pain.

"Leimomi?"

The woman turned, then slowly dragged herself up. She peered at me with violet eyes.

"Corky's alive," Summer said. "I want you to find him."

"Are you OK?" I scanned her body for evidence of abuse. She appeared fine, though from her now even lower-slung burden, it looked like the baby might come any minute.

"Corky didn't die at Waimea." Summer ignored my question. "He's alive. And I need him now." Her voice was still a whisper, but a determined one. She glanced down at her enormous tummy.

I wondered if now was the time to quiz her about her association with Sun. Maybe it didn't matter anymore. She was unharmed and, by the looks of it, at this moment very in need. Besides, she was still my client and I had yet to produce her husband—dead or alive.

"How do you know he's alive?" I asked.

"It's an intuition—a strong intuition."

"OK, for argument sake, let's say that Frank O. Sun did the unthinkable and let Corky live—where do we start looking?"

"Is the surf up?"

I should have thought of that, but I hadn't had a full night's sleep in three days.

"Give me a minute." I opened the door to my office. The familiar mustiness of the place felt reassuring. "What about the baby?" I scanned again her bulging middle.

She grimaced. "I've felt a few small cramps."

"Contractions? Do you need a hospital?"

"Find Corky first. Then I'll go to a hospital."

"Let's talk." I gestured to my client chair. She sat down as I walked behind my desk.

"Somebody has to tell you this, Summer, even at this inopportune time." I paused to gather my thoughts, but there was no gentle way to deliver them. "Corky may not want to see you as much as you want to see him. He thinks your baby isn't his. He thinks it's Damon DiCarlo's."

"This baby is Corky's." Summer stared into my eyes without blinking. "Damon and I never made love. He asked but I refused. I've been faithful to Corky, despite what he thinks. There was never anyone else."

"I believe you." I meant it.

"I think we should go to Waimea Bay." Summer looked at me anxiously. "I want to find Corky before the baby comes."

"You're sure?"

She nodded.

"OK," I sighed. "Back to Waimea."

twenty-three

On the ridge overlooking Waimea Bay I parked my Impala—leaving Summer sprawled in the passenger seat—and began searching for Corky McDahl, again.

Stepping from the car I felt a tug of the Smith & Wesson I had tucked into the right front pocket of my khakis. It felt heavy and cold, and made a bulge in my pants that Summer could have easily noticed, had she been in any condition to look.

I hoped I wouldn't need it. Frank O. Sun had his ice, Summer was free, and Corky was God knows where—on earth or in heaven. Or maybe hell.

So why did I need the revolver? I don't know. I just didn't feel comfortable showing up at Waimea without it.

With my field glasses I scoped out countless surfers in Waimea's lineup. The swell had gone down since this morning. The waves were big enough—twelve to fifteen feet—to attract a crowd, but not too big to frighten anybody off. A half dozen surfers dropped down each precipitous face.

In the unlikely event that Corky actually *was* out there, whose board would he be riding? His own patched candy cane sat safely in my office. I scanned the crowd and managed to pick out Cousin Alika on his sunshine yellow gun and a few of his friends. I also spotted a blond mop head here and there. But nobody who looked like Corky. After searching for several minutes, I gave up and walked back to the car.

"I don't see him," I told Summer.

Hunched over inside the Impala, she glared at me with an intensity that was almost scary.

"Here, let me find him!" She lumbered from the car, reached for the binoculars, and took up a shaky position on the ridge overlooking the bay. I steadied her and suggested she sit down. But she wouldn't.

She swung the field glasses to one side of the lineup, then to the other—coming back again and again to the same spot in the thick of the farthest break.

"Oooohh!" she groaned.

"Are you alright? You should really sit down."

"No." She kept standing, focusing the binoculars. *"That's him,"* she said. "That's Corky. He's on an orange board and he's grown a beard."

"Let me see."

She handed me the glasses and I focused on a bearded blond guy on an orange gun. "Could be," I admitted.

"It *is* him. *Aaahh-Aaahh!*" Summer winced. Her paper white face bore an expression of pure pain.

"Are you—"

"A huge contraction . . ." She grimaced and then buckled over.

"We're finding a hospital." I reached for her hand.

Summer no longer resisted. Inside the car I stretched her out in the front seat, her head on my lap. She was beginning to writhe. *"Aaaaaaahh!-Aaaaaaahh!"*

Neither of us paid anymore attention to the surf or the scenery on the way to Kahuku Community Hospital, about five miles up Kamehameha Highway. By the time we pulled up to the emergency entrance, Summer was breathing fast and hard. I felt totally helpless.

The green-smocked medics wheeled her off in a flash, so I waited. I thought about Leimomi, her pleading voice was echoing in my head. I picked up a *People* magazine and flipped through it without seeing a thing.

Summer delivered a healthy eight-pound, two-ounce baby girl.

"You're the father?" one of the ER nurses said to me in the waiting room.

"Y—" I started to say, then realized where I was. "No, the father is surfing at Waimea Bay."

"Oh . . ." she said.

"Is she OK?" I interrupted any further questioning.

"The mother and daughter are doing fine," the nurse reassured me. "Both are fine."

"Can you tell her I'll be right back?" I stood up. "She'll understand."

"I . . . yes, I can." The nurse looked at me curiously as I turned and made for the door.

I fetched my Impala in the hospital's lot and roared back to Waimea, even faster than the trip over. There was no place to park legally in the bay's lot, so I double parked and walked across the beach, hoping the officer directing traffic was too busy to notice.

Of the dozens of surfers we had seen earlier in the water, a few were now coming in, while others were just paddling out.

I looked around hoping to see someone I knew. Cousin Alika on his yellow board was still in the water. I scanned the faces on the beach.

"Ham!" I said, seeing Alika's surfing buddy. "Get off work fo' check out da surf?"

"Kai, bruddah," Ham said and shook my hand local-style, the Polynesian tattoo on his bicep dancing. "Yeah, I wen' make sandwiches fo' da lunch crowd, den I dig out."

"Ham, you do me one favor?"

"Shoots," he said, tossing his sun-bleached dreadlocks.

"One *haole* guy in da lineup on da orange board—see um?" I pointed.

"Yeah, brah," Ham squinted. "Jus' one orange speck way out dere."

"Dat's him, da California surfah named Corky, you know, da guy dat wipe out Christmas Eve. Tell him come in. If he no come, you round up Alika and da boyz and encourage him, OK?"

"He alive? Da surfah dat wipe out stay alive?"

"Yeah, his wife *hāpai* and jus' deliver one *keiki* at Kahuku Hospital. I goin' drive him down dere."

"Dis guy goin' come in." Ham's serious face looked determined.

"Tanks, 'eh?"

"No mention." Ham mounted his board and paddled into the boiling surf.

I sat on the beach and waited. For the first time since this whole twisted case began, I actually felt peaceful. Summer was alive and well, and so was her baby girl. And Summer's estranged husband, by some miracle I might never understand, was also still alive. I wondered how he might react. Would he believe the child was his? Would he care?

A half hour went by before I saw the orange gun coming in. The closer he got, the more he looked like the photo Summer had brought to Denny's in Waikīkī that rainy Monday morning. Straw yellow hair. Boyish face, and now that blond beard. Not until he walked up the beach could I see his green eyes clearly and understand how both Summer and Maya might have fallen for him. Something about his churlish expression said, "I'm cool."

He scanned the beach with the board under his arm.

"Corky McDahl?" I approached him. He had a totally pissed off look on his face. "Your wife has just given birth to your new daughter."

"Says who?" he blustered with boyhood bravado.

"Kai Cooke." I replied. "I'm the private detective she hired to find you."

"The kid ain't mine." Corky was all attitude. "You got no right to pull me out of the water on such a good day." He turned back toward the waves.

I reached for his arm, but he was already trotting down the beach, heading for the shore break. I ran after him and grabbed a rail of his surfboard.

"Chill!" He yanked away the orange gun. As his toes touched the water, from my khakis I pulled my own gun—the Smith & Wesson.

"Hold on." I pointed it at his head.

"Piss off." He kept walking into the water.

I aimed at his board and fired, ripping a hole through it the size of a silver dollar.

He peered back at me. "You're f–k'n *crazy,* man!"

"Let's go." I pointed the smoldering Smith & Wesson toward my Impala in the parking lot. "I won't hurt you enough to get charged with anything serious, but if I were to drop my gun, say, and it accidentally discharged into your foot, you could miss a lot more than one day of good surf."

Corky scratched his blond mop with the hand that wasn't cradling his damaged board. Then he started walking with me toward my car. A small crowd had gathered around us and followed behind. I figured someone had already dialed 911 by now, so we needed to move fast.

I gestured to the racks on my Impala's teal roof: "Strap your board up there and be quick."

Without snarly comment or surly retort, Corky lifted his surfboard onto my racks. I could see blue sky through that silver dollar-sized hole.

"You drive," I said, as much as I hated turning over the wheel to anybody, especially this guy. "I'll make sure we get there." I held the gun level. Corky climbed into the driver's seat. I shut the door behind me and glanced over my shoulder. No police escorts yet.

Corky didn't say a word during our brief ride. So I decided to break the ice.

"DiCarlo isn't the father, according to your wife. The baby is yours."

Corky didn't respond, his green eyes fixed on the road.

"Look. You and your wife can sort it out. But right now she needs you."

"Like I really care." He kept looking straight ahead.

A few miles from Kahuku Hospital Corky suddenly glanced at me.

"So where's Maya?" he asked.

When I told him she'd flown back to Maui, Corky just shrugged. I had a feeling he was going to leave it that way.

"You're fortunate to be alive," I said, truly curious about his dumb luck. "Why did Sun let you go?"

"I told him where the stuff was hidden," Corky explained.

"I was just at the mission and the ice was gone."

Corky seemed to smile slightly. "I moved it to a locker at the Y before Maya and I split O'ahu."

"So why go to all the trouble to bury a bogus map on Shipwreck Beach?"

"To throw him off. Sun finally realized he could never find the ice without me. So I took him to the Y. He left with the bundle. I left with my life. Not because Sun is generous, but because I convinced him Maya would squeal if anything happened to me."

"Did you know Sun was also holding Summer?"

"I didn't know she was even here." He took a deep breath and a hint of concern spread across his face. Maybe he did actually care. "I'd heard she hired someone to look for me and Maya, but I had no idea she came to Hawai'i herself."

"I think DiCarlo may have brought her against her will. And now he's dead."

"His blood splattered all over me," Corky said, expressionless.

"You know it wasn't an accident. Sun made an example of him. DiCarlo was killed entirely for your benefit."

Corky didn't respond. When we pulled up to the emergency room, I let my Smith & Wesson rest in my lap.

"Just go in. They're expecting you."

Corky eyed the gun, then released his grip on the wheel and looked out the window. Finally he opened the door and let himself out.

I watched the reluctant Californian unlash his orange board, cradle it under his arm, then step slowly into the emergency room. He looked back at me only once.

twenty-four

Back on Maunakea Street I peeked in on the *lei* girls. No Leimomi. *Where was she?*

Upstairs in my office the red light on my answering machine was blinking. I pressed Play.

"Mr. Cooke, this is Meyer Gold, investigator for Acme Life, calling about Charles Corky McDahl, the surfer who died at Waimea Bay last December. Acme has concluded its investigation and is prepared to settle the policy for Mrs. McDahl, who we understand has retained your services. But I'd like to compare notes with you before authorizing the check."

Ho! Mr. Gold was in for a surprise.

I knew who the next message was from even before I heard it.

"Kai? Are you there? Please pick up the phone. Kai . . . ?"

I lifted the receiver before her message ended and dialed Leimomi's number.

"Kai? Is that you?" She answered on the first ring. *"Finally.* Where have you been? I've called your office five times." Leimomi's tone wasn't angry or depressed or even scolding. She just sounded happy to hear from me.

"Sorry, Leimomi—really sorry—it was a case, the California surfer who wiped out at Waimea. The case is over now. I'll be here for you—"

"Kai, the most amazing thing has happened." It was her turn to cut me off.

"What?" I held my breath.

"Daddy is getting out on parole. He's coming home to Kaua'i and I'm going to go there to meet him."

"Well . . . that's great, Leimomi." I was expecting news of her *condition.* "Did your father get out early?"

"Yeah, he's agreed to testify against the drug supplier who got him in trouble."

"I thought your father feared for his life?"

"He did, until the supplier got indicted. It just happened and now Daddy's getting out."

"Wait a minute . . . what's the drug lord's name?"

"Moon or Star or something like that."

"Sun? Frank O. Sun?"

"That's him."

I suddenly recalled my phone message yesterday to Narco-Vice. Could Detective Tong have worked that fast?

"Kai? Are you still there?"

"Uh-huh."

"Anyway, Daddy and Mamma are getting back together. And that leads up to what's so important I wanted to tell you. Kai, I'm sorry, but . . . but I'm not just going to Kaua'i to visit, I'm going back for good. I'm moving home. I miss Daddy and Mamma, and I miss Kaua'i. Honolulu is too big and busy for me—too many people, too much traffic, too much everything."

"Well . . . what about the baby? I mean, what do you want to do?"

"Didn't I tell you?" she said.

"Tell me what?"

"I must have miscounted, or I was just late, or something."

"You said you took the pregnancy test and couldn't bear it alone?"

"No, you didn't listen. I couldn't bear to take the *test* alone. I was afraid of the results. I wanted you with me when I took it . . ."

I was speechless.

"We can still see each other, Kai." Leimomi sounded sympathetic. "You can visit me on Kaua'i. And I could visit sometimes on O'ahu."

"That would be . . . great," I said, still stunned.

"I'm sorry to do this to you. I feel so guilty, leaving you like this. It's not that I don't love you. I do. It's just that I have so much to catch up on with Daddy. I want to be at home for a while."

"Don't feel guilty." If she only knew how much I meant that. "I understand. Can I help you? Give you a ride to the airport? Maybe we could go out to dinner before you leave?"

"I'd like that," she said.

We hung up and I rocked back in my office chair. All that built up emotion. All that reservoir of guilt. All for nothing.

I thought of the ocean blue crystal egg I had bought Leimomi in Makawao. It was the day I discovered Corky was alive, the turning point in the case. I figured the egg would mean more to me than to Leimomi at this point. I dug through my drawers and finally found it, placing it gingerly on my desktop. The turquoise-tinted waves glowed in the sunlight streaming through my office window. A beautiful sight.

I gazed over at Corky's candy cane-striped surfboard lying on a rail against my office wall. After getting my butt kicked the other day at Waimea, I doubted I would ever be riding it. Maybe I could give it to Summer and Corky as a present. Though Corky might not be riding too many more big waves himself. He had become a daddy. And who knows how the drug trial would shake down—whether he would be indicted and, if so, what kind of a plea bargain he might be able to swing.

I spent the rest of the day in a daze, still reeling from Leimomi's surprise announcement and feeling slightly abandoned, both by her and, as much as I hated to admit it, by Maya. I knew it was just my ego, since I didn't really envision a future with either of them. But just the same—those ego beatings can kind of hurt.

Later I wondered if my phone message to Detective Tong, telling all I knew about the Sun organization, could have had any bearing on Sun's indictment or on the early release of Leimomi's father. I doubted it. The wheels of justice turn slowly.

No matter, it was provocative to imagine myself helping to turn those huge wheels.

twenty-five

Monday I took off from work. I counted Sun's sushi-roll of hundreds, glad I had stored it safely in my desk. After expenses—airfare, the lodge, rental cars, and meals—I had cleared nearly three grand.

It took some talking to settle my accounts on Lāna'i. The Jeep Wrangler I rented had to be retrieved from the lodge's parking lot. Late fee, plus an extra day's charge. On the other hand, even though I'd failed to check out at the lodge, the nice folks there were so full of *aloha* that they credited my account for the second night.

When I called the surf line later that day, Waimea had gone down a few feet, but was still pumping. So were Sunset and Pipeline. But the crowds would be out. And I'd been up to the North Shore twice in the last twenty-four hours. Here in town, Waikīkī was breaking two-to-three feet.

I grabbed my longboard and headed for Pops.

Paddling out through Waikīkī's shore break, my arms still felt tight from the other day at Waimea. But after the first few strokes, the stiffness wore away and I felt fine. Truly fine.

I waited in the lineup for a good set. The little swells lifted me up and gently set me down again. They resembled ripples on a pond compared to the thundering mountains up on the North Shore. But I'd had enough of big wave riding for one winter.

HANGING TEN
IN PARIS
A Surfing Detective Novelette

For Miriam and Alan
Who showed me a Paris I'd never seen before
and will never see again.

Acknowledgments

Many thanks once again to my wife Charlene for reading and commenting on *Hanging Ten in Paris,* and for being my partner on life's many journeys. To Stu Hilt, the generous, humble, and brilliant Honolulu private detective who has guided me through every Surfing Detective mystery, this one included. To Christine Matthews for editing an early version of the piece. And to Lorna and Shel Hershinow and Laurie Tomchak for providing invaluable editorial advice. Mahalo to John Michener of Mediaspring for creating the e-book cover and converting the text for digital distribution. And finally to Miriam Fuchs and Alan Holzman, without whom this Surfing Detective mystery would not have been written.

Preface

The idea behind *Hanging Ten in Paris* geminated when I was in that city during the autumn of 2009, after the recent passing of my mother. Though the occasion for this sojourn was to celebrate in grand style the birthday of a dear friend, my mood was understandably somber and I could not shake the dark omnipresence of death. In this atmosphere of sadness and gloom, one evening in a restaurant in the Latin Quarter near the Pantheon I observed a table of a dozen diners—all, except one, American students. The one exception was also an American, a man of at least twice their age. The man could only have been their professor, and their dining together a celebratory event during a study abroad term in Paris.

I knew this scene well because the year before I had taken such a group to study in London. My students all had come from University of Hawai'i, where I taught at the time, some having never before left the islands. As might be expected, a few had problems adjusting to a new culture and a very different climate—it was January when we arrived and spitting snow. My job was to help them through these adjustments and to ensure that each returned to Hawai'i alive and well. All did, thankfully. But I had heard horror stories from previous terms.

Glancing at the dozen students dining together that evening in Paris, my perceptions still clouded by gloom, I began to imagine the worst: What if one of them turned up dead in some tragic and shocking way?

This bleak question followed me through my last days in Paris, until I finally tried to answer it in the form of a Surfing Detective mystery. Then I encountered a problem. Why would Kai Cooke investigate a death in Paris? He didn't speak French. He'd never been to France. And his normal sphere of operations was the six inhabited Hawaiian Islands. My PI was therefore an unlikely detective to take the case.

I was stuck. Until I saw two connections between him and the proposed victim: Ryan Song, like Kai, would be from Hawai'i and he would be a surfer. Then I pieced together a scenario in which Kai would investigate Ryan's death some months later, upon the request of his parents. And due to the Songs' limited means, Kai would conduct his inquiry without ever leaving the islands. No trip to Paris. That meant a challenging case. How would the PI reconstruct a sequence of events that occurred months earlier and seven thousand miles away?

Another, lesser, problem was the matter of length. From the beginning I had conceived the case of Ryan Song as a short story rather than a novel. This would mark, in fact, the first time I had attempted a Surfing Detective mystery in this compact form. When I began to write, the case kept growing and growing—beyond the bounds of the short story, but not reaching the length of the novel, or even the novella. So what did I have—a long story? I was pleased to rediscover the term *novelette,* whose length is midway between the short story and novella.

Novelette describes well *Hanging Ten in Paris.* The advantages of this form are three: it invites us to see Kai Cooke working a case in more depth than we could in a short story; it has the focus and brevity that allows us to read from beginning to end at one sitting; and, finally, it offers those unfamiliar with the series the opportunity to become acquainted, with little time or expense.

one

"What the hell did you do?"

"Get out of my room!" he shouted.

They struggled, knocking over a small table, anger raging as they fell and he landed hard on the floor.

"I told you, we all told you to shut your fat face!"

He didn't answer. He didn't even move. No use talking anymore.

"Oh, my God! Is he dead?"

* * *

"It's Kai Cooke, the Surfing Detective." My arrival was announced by an assistant to Serena Wright, Director of International Studies at Paradise College in Honolulu.

"Quite sad about Ryan," Serena said as I took her hand. I stood almost a foot over her, but what she lacked in stature, she made up in intelligence. She was fortyish, British, and very bright. "I only wish we could put this behind us, Kai."

"The Songs are no doubt grieving," I said as I sat down across from her.

"That's not the problem," she said. "They don't believe Ryan killed himself. And they think that you—a surfer, like Ryan, and a private detective—can somehow prove he didn't. I tried the dissuade them, but it was no use."

"Thanks for the gig," I said.

"Your broad shoulders and sun-bleached hair should convince them you're the genuine article."

I almost said, *And the shark bite on my chest?* But replied: "You're too kind."

She stood, opened a file drawer, and handed me a sheet with color headshots of Ryan and his fellow students from the Paris program—four girls and three guys—seven in all. There was a name under each photo and contact information. Serena pointed to a handsome boy of about twenty with luminous eyes, short spiky hair, and a shy smile. His face was open and sunny.

"That's Ryan," she said.

"Looks like a nice, happy kid," I said.

"He was quiet," she said. "I think that's why he fell for Marie. She's the life of the party." Serena pointed to an attractive island girl with bobbed hair, grey eyes, intelligent brow, and a playful smirk. She looked full of fun.

"Opposites attract," I said.

"Ryan was clever too. His French was the best in the group, next to Marie's, and he played the guitar and had a gorgeous voice. The girls adored him. They took his death very hard. Marie was devastated."

"And the guys?"

"I doubt it was much easier for them. Or for Russ . . . uh, Professor Van."

"What a shame," I said.

"If only Marie hadn't met that fellow Pierre in Paris . . . ." Serena filled me in, then opened her file drawer again and removed a folder labeled RYAN SONG. "Brace yourself, Kai." She handed me a photo.

It was Ryan hanging. He had on a pair of board shorts. No shirt. No shoes. His ten toes appeared to dangle over the floor. His face was almost blue and his head turned at an unnatural angle. Beneath him lay a note and a snapshot of the girl I assumed was Marie. A small table was tipped nearby on its side. The rope around his neck was tied to a chandelier connected to the ceiling by a chain. The photo was stamped: PREFECTURE DE POLICE.

"Sad," I said. But something else was bothering me. Ryan's attire. He looked like any surfer walking down Kalākaua Avenue in Waikīkī. But he was in Paris. In winter. *Board shorts? No shirt or shoes?* I didn't say anything about it, just asked, "How did Ryan get on with the other students?"

"Well," she said, "with everyone." She shook her head. "Here's a copy of the suicide note." It was computer-printed in bold caps: **AU REVOIR, MARIE.**

"I don't speak French," I admitted. "I've never even been to France."

"*Au revoir* means goodbye," Serena said. "You won't have to know any French. And on the Songs' budget, no way you're going to Paris."

"Okay, then why did Ryan print the note? Why not write it by hand?

"Printed in bold caps to make a bold statement?" Serena said.

"Seems kind of impersonal," I said. "Where did you get the note?"

"The college requested Ryan's case file from the Paris police," Serena said. "What was passed on to me is in this folder: The photo, the note, and the police report—translated into English. And here's a DVD about our Paris program and a tourist map." She unfolded on her desk the map displaying major historical sites and buildings.

"So this is Paris?" I gazed at the dizzying maze of streets, each called Rue this or that, and the River Seine that wound through them.

"Our program is at the University of Paris—the Sorbonne—in the Latin Quarter. It's here." She put her finger on a spot just below the river. "On the Left Bank in the Fifth Arrondissement—she pronounced it *ah-rhone-dees-mo*—near the Pantheon, that grand domed building."

"I see it." It was in a square called Place du Panthéon.

"Marie moved into Pierre's apartment on that square," Serena said.

"Is she there now?" I asked.

"No, she's traveling around Europe with him," Serena said. "Anyway, we house our students nearby in a glorious old townhouse divided into flats at forty-four Rue des Écoles."

"Rue des what?"

"Des Écoles"—she pronounced it *days-eh-coal*—"means, roughly, the street of the schools, because the major centers of learning are there. We rent the third and fourth floors. There is a small lift . . . uh, an elevator . . . that stops only on those two floors. Nobody can ride the lift without an ID card—for the safety and security of our students."

"Only your students had cards?"

"Right. And Russ—Professor Van. And the custodial staff."

"So you had seven students on two floors, which only they had access to?"

"Correct. The floors were also connected by a stairway, but only these two floors. Ryan and Marie both started in single rooms on the third. Until she left, of course."

"Convenient," I said.

Serena shrugged. "Two other students, Kim and Heather, close friends and English majors from Oʻahu, shared a double on the third floor."

"And on the fourth?"

"Three more: Meighan, a French major on scholarship from Michigan, in a single room and Brad and Scooter, business majors and football mates from California, in a double. The two mates weren't stellar students, but did well in Russ's French history course, and have since graduated. Actually, all the students did well. I wasn't surprised. We've found studying abroad motivates even less-than-stellar students, and the program tends to draw serious students to begin with. I have Russ's grade records if you'd like to see for yourself."

"Maybe later," I said. "For now, I'd just like to talk to the professor."

"He's beastly busy right at present, but I'm sure he'll oblige," she said. "He's applying for the Hilo Hattie Chair. It means more money and less teaching. He's competing against his bitter rival, Professor Blunt from American Studies." She raised her brows. "High stakes."

"I'll wish Professor Van luck," I said, but wondered about a teacher who didn't want to teach.

"Do me a favor, Kai. When you talk to Russ and the students—and especially to Ryan's parents—tread lightly. We've had enough sadness already."

I repeated her admonition: "Tread lightly."

We talked about Ryan for a few more minutes. Then I walked back to my car in the blazing summer sun.

two

From Serena's office I drove through Waikīkī and saw some nice sets rolling in. Before long I had my board in the water and I was paddling to Pops, or Populars, about a quarter mile offshore from the Sheraton. Pops was cranking—typical of a summer swell. The right-breaking curls seemed to sweep from here to eternity. You can tuck into those curls and ride your cares away.

Suicide wasn't my favorite kind of case, especially when the deceased was so young. I didn't relish the prospect of meeting Ryan's parents later that afternoon. That's why I couldn't pass by Waikīkī. Besides, Serena had mentioned that Pops was Ryan's favorite spot in town. Could surfing here give me insights into his character? And into the case? I hoped so. The facts I'd been given so far made me doubt I could tell the Songs much more than they already knew.

A wave on the horizon caught my eye. I stroked into position and took it—a nice one about shoulder high. I tucked into the curl and screamed along.

Paddling back to the lineup, I thought about Ryan. Serena told me he'd been sweet on Marie since high school and apparently hoped their friendship would blossom into romance in Paris. But a few weeks after they arrived for the spring term, Marie met a student at the University of Paris. In what seemed to her friends like a very short time, she and Pierre were living together. Ryan was stung. Far from home and family—Hawai'i was half way around the world—he succumbed to his despair.

The night he died was February 29, Marie's twenty-first birthday. She was a leap-year baby. And it turned out she and Pierre had been far from Paris when it happened, celebrating at his parents' home in Lyons. That was the official version of the story, anyway.

I wondered about Ryan killing himself by hanging. No surfer I knew of had ever done that. Surfers who die before their time usually get swallowed by a wave or a shark, or by the drugs that have invaded surfing culture. Wave riders go down doing what they love. Or they just go down. A surfer hanging himself would be rare. But Ryan was in Paris when he died and had no waves to chase his blues away. Would a landlocked surfer in despair take his own life?

As many waves as I rode at Pops that morning, none gave me an answer.

three

I showered at Queen's Surf Beach, toted my board back to my car in the Honolulu Zoo lot, put on my street clothes, and headed up Kapahulu Avenue to St Louis Heights. The Songs' home was near the top of the sloping ridge overlooking Waikīkī's skyline. The air up there was cooler. And the sky bluer. I pulled up in front of their island-style bungalow, squeezed between two McMansions that made their place look like servants' quarters. Neat and tidy, but not fancy. In front stood a mango tree that Ryan no doubt climbed as a boy, and a dusty pickup with signs that said SONG MASONRY CONTRACTING.

I stepped across the close-clipped grass to a covered *lānai* and knocked on the door. A handsome part-Hawaiian woman greeted me. She had the same luminous eyes and shy smile as her son. But the smile could not mask the sadness in her face.

"Come in," she said, looking too young to be the mother of a twenty-year-old.

The living room continued the neat and tidy theme: rattan couch and chairs and coffee table, a few lamps, and an area rug. Except for a surfboard mounted like a trophy on one wall, which I took to be Ryan's, that was it. And a guitar leaning against another wall. Also his?

"Lono!" she called into a bedroom. A deeply-tanned local man ambled into the living room. He was wiry—all muscle and bone.

"Sorry about your son." I shook Mr. Song's hand. It was warm but callused hard like concrete.

"My son nevah wen' kill himself," he said in Pidgin. "Nevah!"

"Lono . . ." His wife tried to calm him.

"My family name been ruin by dis lie!" Mr. Song's face reddened.

"Why don't we sit down," Ryan's mother said, her shy smile fading.

We sat and Mrs. Song said, "Ryan was a serious boy, Mr. Cooke. He didn't always put himself forward, but he was not weak. I know my own boy. I know he would never do this to his father and me."

"Was no coward!" Mr. Song cried. "My son nevah—" He buried his face in his hands.

"I'm sorry, sir," I said again. I'm sure he didn't hear me.

Mrs. Song kept her composure. "Ryan was sad when Marie went off with that French boy, but he didn't take it so hard as everyone thinks."

"How do you know?" I asked.

"He sent me emails," she said. "He said, 'I'm OK, Mom. Paris is cool.' He said he was seeing the sights with a girl named Meighan who lived on the next floor."

"Do you still have the emails?"

"Yes. And we have Ryan's laptop. The college mailed it along with his things. Do you want to take it?"

"Sure." I had no idea what use the laptop might be, but with so little to go on I couldn't afford to pass.

"I'll get it for you before you leave," she said.

We talked at length about Ryan's relations with friends, family, and other students, and his frame of mind before he left for France. Then I asked, "Could Ryan have said he was okay just so you wouldn't worry?"

"We tell da truth in dis family." Mr. Song uncovered his tear-streamed face. "Jus' prove he nevah do 'em."

"Honey . . . ." His wife put her hand on his shoulder.

"Are you sure you want me to investigate?" I looked into his pained eyes.

They both nodded.

"Okay, I'll need a retainer to get started," I said. "Five hundred should do for now." That was half my usual.

Mrs. Song disappeared and then returned with a rusty Spam can. She pulled out a wad of crumpled bills, flattening them one by one on the coffee table. She counted to five hundred.

I took the bills, but didn't feel good about it.

"One last thing." I suddenly remembered something that was bothering me. "Why did Ryan take board shorts to France?"

"He planned to surf at a place called Biarritz," Mrs. Song said.

"Sure, maybe that explains it," I replied.

We exchanged goodbyes, Mrs. Song gave me Ryan's laptop, and I left.

Walking to my car I realized that while Ryan's intending to surf Biarritz explained why he brought board shorts to France, it didn't explain why he had them on when he died. So I still had a problem.

four

Returning to my Waikīkī Edgewater studio that night I unfolded the map of Paris Serena had given me and studied the dizzying array of streets and the river that wove through them. Why Parisians called one bank of the Seine right and the other left didn't make sense to me. The orientation looked more north and south. But eventually I found the Left Bank and the Latin Quarter. A 5^E was printed smack in the middle. That meant nothing to me, so I Googled it.

> 5ème – Fifth Arrondissement –This neighborhood, the fabled Latin Quarter, takes its name from the Sorbonne, where Latin was the common tongue for all students during the Middle Ages. The neighborhood has the feel of a small village and students mix freely with professionals in its winding streets. Ernest Hemingway and James Joyce lived here, and many other writers, artists, and philosophers . . . .

Not a bad start. Next I located the domed Pantheon and remembered Serena saying Ryan and his fellow students lived nearby on Rue des Écoles. I found it and also the cross street she had mentioned as an afterthought: Rue Thénard. I drew a circle around the intersection.

So I had it. The very spot where Ryan Song had died.

Hoping to see the actual building, I slipped the disk Serena gave me into my DVD player. The program began with a brassy version of the French national anthem—same as the horn opening to the Beatles' "All You Need is Love." The major monuments and tourist attractions of Paris flashed by on the screen. And in case I might miss any of them, a sonorous voiceover identified each. Then the pitch began:

> *Paradise College, International Studies Division, welcomes you to Paris. Imagine living and studying in this world famous city most people only dream of visiting. Paris, the city of lights. Paris, the city of love. That's you atop the Eiffel Tower! That's you admiring the Mona Lisa at the Louvre. That's you in a sidewalk café watching the glamour of Parisian life stroll by. It's a once-in-a-lifetime opportunity, and it can be yours!*

Sign me up—I was sold already. Soon the narrator got to student accommodations.

> *You will live in an historic Eighteenth-Century town home, apportioned into single and double rooms expressly for Paradise College students, at the illustrious address: 44 Rue des Écoles . . . .*

I froze the image. It *was* an elegant building—six stories, by my count—with a Mansard roof, brick chimneys, tall windows, wrought iron balconies, and blooming planters. On the ground floor was a florist called *L'ile aux Fleur* that reminded me of the flower lei shop beneath my office. Only more chic.

I pressed PLAY and the video continued with course options, excursions, and the school calendar, concluding with another round of Paris images. I kept waiting for the price tag. But it never came. The sonorous voice merely said, "A semester in Paris is more affordable than you might imagine . . ." And that was it.

I ejected the DVD and turned to the police report. Paris Police had a more elegant way of saying a young man had hung himself than Honolulu Police did. The English translation, sprinkled with French phrases, said the American student had taken his own life as a result of feelings of dejection and despair over his spurned love for a beautiful young woman. And he had done so fittingly and symbolically on the evening of her birthday. The suicide note—AU REVOIR, MARIE—and her photo seemed to provide evidence *irréfutable*. A summary of statements by Ryan's professor and fellow students corroborated this. The fact that Ryan had apparently taken the rope *impulsivement*—impulsively, I guessed—from a maintenance room in the building further suggested his desperation. He was pronounced dead at the scene at four minutes after nine on Wednesday morning, March first. It was estimated that death occurred the night before, on February twenty-ninth, no later than ten o'clock. Considering the absence of other motives, and after interviews with persons who might shed light on the incident *regrettable*, the case was closed.

five

The next morning I drove to the Kakaʻako campus of Paradise College to interview Professor Russell Van, whose cramped office smelled of pipe tobacco and musty books. He extended a cool pink palm with the grip of a gummy bear, so unlike the warm firm hand of Ryan's father. The professor pointed to a chair and I sat.

"You're here about Ryan?" he said with a hint of nervousness in his voice. His double chin and aloha shirt blousing around his belly revealed a plumpness I'd thought was no longer in fashion in the academy. But Professor Van was obviously an old-timer.

I nodded. "I read the summary of your statement to the Paris police and hoped your wouldn't mind telling me what happened in your own words."

"So his parents don't think he did it?" the professor said. "Let me tell you, I saw him hanging there over the snapshot of her. How can there be any doubt?"

I shrugged. "Did you talk with him before it happened?"

"When Marie moved in with that French student, it bothered Ryan. He just wasn't himself. I emailed Serena and she said to call him in."

"Did you?"

"I did. Ryan said little. Just that he'd be okay. He really didn't want to talk about it."

"Did you talk with him again?"

"No—" Van hesitated. "Well, he did come to see me a few days later. But not about Marie. About something else."

"What?"

"It was unrelated. So I didn't even mention it to the police." Van rocked back uneasily in his chair. "He said he wanted to discuss the next exam."

"Was he worried about his grade?"

"I doubt it. He was carrying an A-minus. Anyway, I'll never know. I was on my way to a lecture on the medieval French *ballade* when he came in. I told Ryan I'd be back in an hour, but he didn't return. The next time I saw him was on that awful morning."

"Would you mind telling me what you saw?"

"When I got there all the students—except Marie, of course—were standing outside Ryan's door. He was hanging very still."

"How did the students react?"

"Meighan was crying. But the others just looked dumbstruck."

"Is that what you expected?"

"When you take these island kids to a place like Paris, you don't know what to expect." He arched his woolly brows. "For many, it's their first time away from Hawai'i. Some handle it, others don't."

"Did they handle it?"

"For the most part. All seven took my French history course, which included excursions to the Bastille, Versailles, et cetera. So I got to know them fairly well. I usually teach the course as a large lecture with standardized exams. But this was a small, intimate group. To keep the course on par I used the same exams, but otherwise I ran it like a seminar."

"Did Ryan spend time with anybody besides Marie?"

"Sometimes with Meighan. Sometimes with Kim and Heather."

"What about Brad and Scooter?"

"I was told the guys went to the *Folies Bergère* together. But Brad and Scooter's appetite—and budget—for cabarets apparently exceeded Ryan's. Not to mention Brad's appetite for the dancers."

"The two guys partied *and* got good grades?"

"When you're twenty you can do things us older folks can't." Van rocked forward in his chair.

"And Marie—what was she like?"

"One of my best students ever. An A-plus. I rarely give those."

"I never saw one," I said. "But, if I care to see hers, Serena said I could look at your grade records."

"Don't bother. They won't tell you anything about Ryan you don't already know." The professor frowned. "I'll never teach in Paris again. What happened there ruined it for me. I haven't slept well since, even with the little pills my doctor gave me. Best to stay here and finish my book, anyway."

"To help your chances for the Hilo Hattie Chair? To help you defeat your bitter rival, Professor Blunt?"

Van looked surprised. "How did you know?"

"Serena told me." I stood and thanked him. "Good luck winning that Chair, sir."

He let out a breath as I left his office, seeming relieved the interview was over. Why? Whatever could make the professor anxious if he were so sure Ryan had taken his own life?

six

From Paradise College I stopped by the Waikīkī Edgewater and sent identical emails to the five students I planned to interview on Oʻahu. I sent a different email to Marie, who Serena had said was traveling in Europe. The email to Marie contained questions; the emails to the others contained a request to meet.

Moments later, a reply arrived from meighan616@pc.edu: "I'm still very sad about Ryan but will try to talk with you. Call me. Meighan McMannis."

She had been first to find Ryan hanging, according to Serena, so it seemed apropos to interview her first.

I called Meighan and arranged to meet her at a Starbucks near Ward Centre. She said she was taking a summer course in French and would stop by after class.

I was sipping a decaf when the green-eyed Michigan blonde stepped in, toting her French textbook. She was no frail flower, but a solid, sturdy young woman who looked as if she could endure those frigid Midwestern winters. She ordered a large latte and joined me. The animated conversations going on around us assured me we wouldn't be overheard.

"Ryan was a sweet guy." Meighan fixed her green eyes on me and sipped her latte. "I loved him."

I said nothing. Just waited.

"I mean, it's not like that." She seemed surprised at what she had said. "He was just a good, gentle soul."

"You said in your statement that you were the first to find Ryan. Can you tell me how that happened?"

"Sure. Heather called and asked me to check on Ryan. She hadn't seen him and was worried. So I went down to his room. The door was unlocked."

"You lived on the fourth floor, right? And Heather and Kim lived on the third, same as Ryan?"

She nodded.

"Why didn't Heather check on him herself?"

"I don't know. She just asked if I'd mind and I didn't. So I went."

"What time?"

"About eight on Wednesday morning. I knocked on his door. There was no answer. I knocked again and then tried the knob. The door opened. I saw him."

"Did you go into the room?"

"Not really." She gripped her coffee. Her hands trembled. "It was kind of . . . uh, a shock. And I didn't want to disturb anything."

"So you did or didn't go into his room?"

"I didn't." Her eyes glistened. "Look, I'm only trying to help Ryan's mom and dad. But I feel like you're accusing me."

"Sorry," I said, then pressed on. "What did you do after you saw Ryan?"

"I banged on Heather and Kim's door. I was crying. They knew right away something was wrong. All three of us walked back to Ryan's room and I opened the door again."

"How did Heather and Kim react?"

"Heather gasped and said, 'Oh, my God!' or something like that. Kim asked, 'What should we do?'"

"I said we should call the police. Heather said we should call Professor Van first. And that's what we did."

"Why call the professor before the police?"

"I don't know. It wasn't my idea. But Heather insisted."

"Where were Brad and Scooter when all this was happening?"

"I was coming to that. They sometimes partied all night and then slept in the next day. We didn't know if we should wake them. But Heather said—'Let's get 'em.' So she and I walked upstairs and knocked on their door. I was surprised when it opened right away."

"They weren't hung over—sleeping it off?"

"Brad looked better than Scooter, who'd obviously been drinking. But Brad said they both had a test that morning and had stayed up studying. We took them down to Ryan's room."

"And how did Brad and Scooter react?"

"Brad covered his face. Scooter just stared with a kind of wonder in his eyes. Then Professor Van showed up and walked into Ryan's room, looked around, and called the police. When they came, we had to leave the building and wait down on the sidewalk. An officer who spoke English came down and interviewed each of us separately. By the time they let us back upstairs, Ryan had been taken away."

"And you didn't go back into his room after that?"

"No, not after they took him away."

Meighan had contradicted herself. First she said she hadn't gone into Ryan's room, and then she implied she had. Either she was confused or withholding information.

I asked her more questions about what happened that night, what led up to it, and what followed. Before long nearly an hour had passed. I finished my decaf and said, "Can I give you a ride back to campus?"

"Nah, I'll just stay here and study my French."

I stood and said the only French I knew. *"Au revoir."*

She sat bolt upright.

"What's wrong?"

"The note," she said. "Ryan's suicide note."

seven

I drove to my office on the corner of Maunakea and Beretania Streets in Chinatown. I'm on the second floor above Fujiyama's Lei Shop. The sweet aroma of fresh plumeria *lei* being strung inside the shop followed me up the stairs—assuaging, in some way, the sad business I'd gotten myself into. Unlocking my door, I glanced at the longboard rider and SURFING DETECTIVE: CONFIDENTIAL INVESTIGATIONS—ALL ISLANDS airbrushed there and wondered again why I was investigating a suicide in Paris. *Ryan was a surfer.* That was the best I could do.

I checked my emails: I had new ones from Heather and Scooter. Heather said I could meet her and her friend Kimberly at Magic Island that afternoon. Scooter said he could see me at the Outback Steakhouse in Hawai'i Kai the next day. I confirmed both interviews, then later headed to Magic Island.

Heather and Kimberly were sitting on a bench by the seawater lagoon when I pulled up. Magic Island is not really an island, but a grassy peninsula on the Diamond Head end of Ala Moana Beach Park with the lagoon at the point. Beyond that is a sea wall and crashing surf.

The two twenty-something island girls were in running gear—tank tops, shorts, and trainers. Heather had long black hair, soft curves, and a fuller, more luxuriant figure than her friend's. Kimberly, by contrast, was lean and small-breasted and pony-tailed. They told me they both worked at a boutique at Ala Moana Shopping Center, not far from their apartment on Pi'ikoi Street.

After a few pleasantries, I asked Heather: "Why did you ask Meighan to look in on Ryan? Why not just walk across the hall yourselves?"

There was silence for a moment. Kim swung her ponytail around and gave Heather a look that said, *Say something!*

"I did," Heather leaned toward me, her gaping top revealing more of her ample breasts than a newly-met man ought to see. "Kim and I both did," she said. "But Ryan didn't answer. So we went back to our room and called Meighan."

"Why not just open Ryan's door? Hadn't you done that before?"

"Yeah, but this time it didn't feel right." Heather again. "We thought Ryan was with someone."

"Who? Not Marie. She was miles away."

"Meighan." Kim finally chimed in.

"Meighan?" I must have sounded surprised. Kim covered her mouth.

Heather gave her a look and then to me said, "It's no secret Meighan liked Ryan. When Marie left, Meighan kind of . . . well, made her move."

As my interview with the two friends progressed, I compared what they said with their statements in the police report, and also with the version of events already supplied by Professor Van and Meighan. It quickly became clear that Kim was the sidekick and Heather called the shots. All the time the latter was talking, something was bugging me. I'd gotten the same feeling listening to Meighan and the professor. While their statements were all uncannily consistent, something was being left out. What?

I asked several more questions—with the same results. Finally, I said: "You can speak freely to me. I'm not the police. I'm just trying to help out Ryan's mom and dad. And I'm not suggesting either of you did anything wrong."

Kim looked pale. Heather piped up: "We are speaking freely. We've told you everything."

"Mahalo," I said. But my reply was hardly more sincere than hers. Heather and Kim had told me almost nothing. But from their evasions and omissions came a clearer message than they intended. "If you happen to think of anything else," I handed both of them my card, "would you please call or email?"

They nodded.

I stood and turned toward my car, then turned back again and said, "Oh, one last thing. Do either of you know any reason why someone might want to harm Ryan?"

The two friends looked startled. Predictably it was Heather who spoke. "Why would you ask such a question?"

"Sorry, I have to."

"Then all I can say," Heather responded, "is not really. Ryan was a super nice guy."

"So I've heard."

I walked back to my car wondering what these Paradise College students and their professor weren't telling me.

eight

The next day I got an email from Marie. She said in a P.S. she was in Stuttgart, Germany, and heading for Heidelberg.

```
Dear Kai,
    It's so sad about Ryan.  I really miss him.
    Yes, the police report was correct.  I was
away from Paris when Ryan died.  An officer
interviewed me after I returned.  I'm afraid
I wasn't very helpful because I hadn't really
talked much with Ryan since early February.
    I sent him an email then trying to explain
about Pierre.  I told Ryan he would always
be a dear friend.  And that I hoped he would
understand.  We didn't talk much after that.
    I still feel terrible about what happened.
He was such a sweet guy.  Everybody liked him.
I can't think of anyone who didn't.
    Please send my condolences to Ryan's parents
and let me know if you have more questions.

    Aloha, Marie
```

I didn't see the need, at that point, to question Marie further. A girl who's broken a guy's heart has little reason to wish him further harm. If she has a conscience, as Marie apparently had, she feels badly enough already. So unless Marie was an accomplished liar and unless the others were covering for her—highly unlikely—there wasn't much reason to suspect her of anything other than the bad timing of Ryan turning up dead on her twenty-first birthday.

nine

That afternoon I drove to the Outback Steakhouse in Hawai'i Kai to interview Scooter. The restaurant was perched on Kalaniana'ole Highway across from Maunalua Bay and flanked by the twin volcanic mounds of Koko Head and Koko Crater. Walking to the restaurant from my car I watched a windsurfer etch a frothy white trail across the bay and remembered that I hadn't heard from Scooter's buddy, Brad. I would ask about that.

A big guy with curls framing his baby-boy face smiled when I asked for Scooter. I should have looked at his nametag. He had fifty pounds on me, easy. I recalled Serena saying Scooter and his pal Brad had played high school football together. We sat in the empty waiting room during the lull between lunch and dinner.

Scooter removed his server apron with meaty paws and said, "Too bad about Ryan." His voice was soft for such a large man. And he sounded almost sincere.

"Too bad," I said.

He then gave me a version of the same story I'd heard before. It was consistent with his earlier statement, but like the other students, he sounded rehearsed. Somewhere near the end of his spiel he said he hadn't gone into Ryan's room on the night he died.

"But you did go into Ryan's room at other times?" I asked.

"Yeah, hanging out. We hung out in each other's rooms."

Hanging? Hung? Scooter seemed oblivious to his inappropriate choice of words. But I said nothing and pressed on.

"Professor Van said you and Brad hit some clubs with Ryan," I carried on, "but you didn't do much with him after that. How come?"

"We were into different stuff—that's all."

"I'm curious, Scooter"—I shifted gears—"why does a business major with no background in French go to Paris and study French history?"

"I dunno." He looked bewildered. "A buddy of ours took Professor Van's course and liked it, so Brad and I decided—why not go to Paris?"

"Just like that?"

"Yeah . . . well, we had to apply and get financial aid, but—"

"You didn't have trouble with the language?"

"Not really. They spoke English in the courses we took."

"Serena said you did well in Professor Van's course."

"Uh . . . 'cause I liked it, I guess."

"No doubt," I said. "Say, do you know how I can get in touch with Brad? He didn't answer my email."

"Yeah, he's working in Waikīkī at the Moana Surfrider—front desk." Scooter rattled off Brad's number.

Finally I asked if Scooter knew of anyone who might want to hurt Ryan, and got the same response I had from the others—a startled look and the professed disbelief that such a fine person could be harmed by another.

Leaving the restaurant, I turned back and saw Scooter pulling out his cell phone. He was calling Brad to tip him off that I was coming. So I waited.

By the time I got back to my car, I tried Brad. He didn't sound surprised to hear from me. And he didn't sound enthusiastic when he agreed to meet at the Surfrider.

ten

I parked at the foot of Diamond Head and walked down oceanfront Kalākaua Avenue into Waikīkī. The Surfrider was the first hotel on the beach. A balmy breeze wafted through the open-air lobby. Beyond it, tourists glistened on the white sand and bobbed in the turquoise sea. Two clerks were working the desk—a redheaded girl and a tall guy with ice-blue eyes. Brad had the looks of a TV anchorman and the physique of an NFL all-star. Even in his hotel uniform he looked powerful. A tight end to Scooter's lineman.

We shook hands and Brad said: "I can talk until we get traffic at the desk." He turned to the redhead. "Uh, this is Amber."

Amber said, "Hi."

So we got the formalities out of the way and moved beyond her earshot.

"Really too bad about Ryan," Brad said, sounding like his buddy.

"Too bad," I said again. It was becoming my automatic response.

"His death hit us all hard," Brad continued, "and kind of pulled us together."

"How's that?"

Just then a twenty-something in a dripping bikini glided up to the desk. His eyes locked on her. I remembered Van's commenting on Brad's appetite for cabaret dancers. But the bikini went to Amber. A shadow crossed his face.

"Look, I shouldn't tell you," he bent toward me and lowered his voice, "but you'll probably find out anyway."

"Tell me what?" I asked.

"About Heather and me. We started up a kind of thing in Paris."

"And?"

"Well . . . man, she's pregnant!"

I tried to keep a straight face. Then I remembered the extra flesh Heather was carrying. *Could be.*

"Her roommate doesn't even know," he said. "It wasn't exactly planned."

"Why are you telling me this?" I was curious. "Does it have anything to do with Ryan?"

"No, but you're a detective. You'd find out about Heather and me anyway. I'm telling you the truth about us so you'll know I'm telling the truth about Ryan."

I shrugged. "Okay, so tell me."

Then he started in on the same story Scooter and the others had told. And, like them, he sounded canned. He stuck almost precisely to his statement in the police report. Often people alter something, if ever so slightly, in the retelling. But Brad's reprise was dead on. I just let him talk. The more he thought I believed him, the better my chances to gain his cooperation later, if necessary.

When I asked if he knew anyone who might want to hurt Ryan, Brad said the only person he could think of was Marie.

"I meant bodily harm," I said. "Do you think Marie was capable of that?"

Brad shrugged. "She sure could have thought more about Ryan's feelings."

"I suppose."

I asked Brad several more questions, he answered them halfheartedly, and then I walked back to my car, sorting out what he had said. Why had he told me Heather was pregnant? And why had he pointed suspicion at Marie? Brad seemed smart enough not to simply blurt these things out—unless he had a reason.

eleven

I drove to Starbucks, ordered a decaf, and waited. It was about the same time I had interviewed Meighan the previous day. If she was a creature of habit, like most people, she'd show up before long.

No sooner had I sat down with my coffee than the Michigan blonde pushed open the door, walked to the counter, and ordered a latte. When it was ready she turned to look for a table. I stood and waved.

"What a surprise," I said. "Do you come here often?"

"Funny," Meighan said, "I didn't think you were much of a coffee drinker."

"I'm not," I said.

She gave me a look.

"As long you're here, what do you say we talk a bit more about Ryan? You know, just to clear up loose ends."

"Fine." She glanced down at her latte; the aroma made me wish I'd ordered one.

"You said Heather asked you to check on Ryan. Right?"

"That's right." She sipped her latte.

"Then you went down to his room, the door was open, and you walked in."

She nodded and took another sip.

"Then what?"

"I saw Ryan hanging and then I ran and got Heather and Kim."

"But what did you do *inside* his room?"

"I didn't go in."

"But you just said you did."

She turned away. "I don't want to talk about it."

"Look, Meighan, if Paradise College finds out you withheld information about Ryan's death, you don't want to know the consequences." It was an empty threat, but the best I could come up with.

She sat in silence, sipping her latte and apparently weighing what I had said. I had no idea which way she'd go. The defiance in her eyes suggested I'd lost the battle. But suddenly her look softened and she said, "Okay, I did find Ryan hanging in his room, but not like everybody thinks. He was naked."

"Naked—as in nude?"

She nodded.

"No board shorts?" My instincts about his attire were apparently right.

"He had nothing on." Meighan gripped her cup. "I didn't want him to be found that way, so I slipped on the shorts."

"You weren't embarrassed seeing him naked, or squeamish touching his skin?"

"Well, no"—she blushed—"I'd, uh, seen him before."

"You had?" *If Meighan had been intimate with Ryan after Marie left, maybe he wasn't as brokenhearted as everybody but his own mother was saying?* I kept that thought to myself.

"I'd rather not go into it." Meighan looked away.

"Okay, then what happened?"

She faced me again. "I left the room. And when I came back with the others, I didn't say anything about the board shorts."

"Did Heather or Kim say anything beyond what you already told me?"

"Not much. Well . . . Kim whispered to Heather. And then Heather put her finger to her lips."

"And what did you make of that?" I knew the answer but I wanted to hear it from her.

"That they already knew Ryan had hung himself?"

I left my decaf on the table on my way out.

twelve

A crack had opened in the wall of deceit. Concerned that Meighan might talk to Heather and Kim, I drove immediately to their apartment. I parked in view of their second-floor flat at the Pi'ikoi Arms, a faded, low-rise slab building near Ala Moana Center. I called their number. No answer. It was around the time they'd come home from their jobs. I trusted my stake-out wouldn't last long.

I was wrong. I waited a half hour. Then another. I was about to pack it in when Heather strolled by and climbed the stairs. I let her go. I didn't want her—I wanted her sidekick. I waited. Kim eventually walked by and I popped out of my car.

"What are you doing here?" She looked curious, even cracked a smile.

"I was in the neighborhood and was worried about you."

"Worried about *me*? Why?"

"Because you don't deserve to go down for Ryan's death. I doubt you had anything to do with it. But you're putting yourself at risk by sticking with your friends who did."

"What do you mean? Ryan committed suicide."

"Take a deep breath, Kim, and please listen to reason."

She stood silently.

"You and Heather knew Ryan was dead that morning before you asked Meighan to check on him."

Her smile faded. "It wasn't my idea."

"I know, but why pretend to have Meighan find him?"

"Heather knocked and Ryan didn't answer," Kimberly explained. "But we figured he was there because I'd heard noise in his room at about nine the night before."

"What kind of noise?"

"Like furniture moving."

"Heather didn't hear it?"

"She wasn't there. Heather had a stomachache that night and went to the pharmacy."

It wasn't a stomachache, I thought. But Kim didn't need to know her roommate was pregnant until Heather was ready to tell her.

"So what really happened the next morning?" I asked.

"When Ryan didn't answer we opened the door and saw him hanging. And I guess we just got scared."

"Scared of what?"

"Of finding him like that." She shrugged.

"C'mon, Kim, I'm trying to keep you out of trouble—but you have to cooperate and tell me the truth."

"Believe me," she said, "I had nothing to do with it. I liked Ryan. I would never dream of hurting him."

"I know you wouldn't hurt Ryan. But somebody did. I need to know who and why."

"I told you, I don't know."

"I think you do. You can tell me or you can tell HPD."

Another empty threat, but she thought it over.

"Kim?" I coaxed her. "What's it going to be?"

She hesitated, then finally opened her mouth and the words tumbled out: "I think Ryan's death might have had something to do with cheating."

"Cheating on who?"

"Not cheating on a person. Cheating on exams."

"Whose exams?"

"Professor Van's."

"Ryan cheated?" That didn't sound like him.

"Not Ryan. He caught someone with the answers to all the exams. I don't want to say who . . . ." She hesitated. "Ryan didn't think it was fair for this person to party while the rest of us worked."

Most college students party. The seven who went to Paris would be no exception. But only two of them were reputed party animals. It would most likely be one or the other, or both. I didn't press Kim. I didn't need to. But I did ask: "Why do you think Ryan's death had to do with this cheating?"

"He told the person to stop or he'd go to Professor Van."

"Did the person stop?"

"No."

"Then why didn't Ryan go to the professor?" I recalled that Van had said nothing to me about cheating.

"Ryan did go to Professor Van."

"He did?" *Was Van involved too?*

"Yeah, Ryan told me the Prof. would speak to us about it."

"Did Professor Van speak to you?"

"Not to me or Heather."

"Did he speak to anyone? Did he do anything?"

She shrugged. "I don't know."

Before I could respond, she ran into the Pi'ikoi Arms crying, *"Shit! Heather's going to kill me!"*

thirteen

First thing the next morning I took up Serena on her offer to see the professor's grade computations. I couldn't help wondering about Van. Why had he apparently done nothing to stop the alleged cheating? Why had he withheld information from the college and the Paris police? And from me?

I picked up a large brown envelope from Serena's assistant and opened it as I stepped back into the morning sun. Inside was a single sheet with the names of the seven students and columns displaying exam scores, semester averages, and letter grades. What immediately stuck me as odd was that all seven—except Ryan, of course—finished the term with an A. There were a few minuses and one plus—for Marie, as Van had told me—but no grade less than A. Not one B. Not one C. How often does that happen in an undergraduate course?

I checked the students' individual exam scores and found, not to my surprise, that both Brad and Scooter—the business major-party animals—had the highest marks in French History next to Marie's. From one exam to the next, a few points separated the two. But their scores, otherwise, followed a nearly identical pattern. Then I remembered two things: Van telling me he used the same exams in Paris as he had in Hawai'i; and Scooter telling me a friend had taken Van's course in a previous term. *Bingo*: Scooter got the exams from his friend and brought them to Paris.

Then I noticed something else curious. Heather's and Kim's scores began in the 70s, but about mid-way through the term, when Ryan had died, their scores rose nearly twenty points into the 90s. Did they suddenly start studying? When I checked their grades for the later part of the term against Brad and Scooter's, I found the same pattern. Mulling it over, Heather's and Kim's dramatic improvement made sense. If Heather and Brad were lovers, he would naturally share the exams with her. And Heather would share them with her friend Kim.

But what I wasn't prepared for were Meighan's scores. Hers started higher than those of the other girls—fitting for a scholarship student—then shot up even further about mid-term, following the same pattern. *Were they* all *cheating?*

Not the best and brightest of the bunch. Not Ryan's unrequited love, Marie. Her A-plus clearly distinguished her from the others. But, just to be thorough, I checked her record. Marie's scores began exceptionally high. On the first exam she hit 98 percent. On the second, a perfect 100. She stood head and shoulders above the pack. When I scanned her scores to mid-term, my jaw dropped. They continued high—but took on the same pattern as Brad's, Scooter's, and the others. Had she quit studying and started coasting? Why would a brilliant student, who could earn an A-plus on her own, cheat?

Ryan knew the answer. But he was no longer alive to tell.

fourteen

Later that afternoon I paddled back out to Pops—Ryan's favorite break. The waves were rolling in three to four feet. Traffic was light. It was a weekday and the regulars hadn't gotten off work yet. I got a couple of rides. Then I waited between sets—and tried to put together the pieces I'd gathered on the case.

Kim had told the truth about the cheating. But she had failed to mention that not just one person was cheating—the entire class was cheating. Herself included. If Professor Van couldn't see it, he was blind. Or had he turned a blind eye?

All seven students had lied. Their professor had, at minimum, withheld information and abdicated his responsibilities to them and to the college. Were they covering for each other—all of them involved in Ryan's death?

fifteen

Back in my Waikīkī apartment that night I checked the mail program on Ryan's laptop. Oddly, I found no personal messages from early February before he had died, only generic and junk emails. What puzzled me more was that I found not even the emails between Ryan and his mother that she had mentioned. These personal messages might have revealed Ryan's state of mind—and also contributing factors to his death. In other words, they were essential.

Then I realized that since Ryan had been a long way from home—in Paris, not in Honolulu—he would have used webmail rather than his laptop's mail program, connected no doubt to a Honolulu server. With a little searching I found his webmail link. The inbox looked identical to the other. No personal emails. All had apparently been deleted. Then I remembered that deleting messages from webmail doesn't necessarily remove them. Deleted emails go to a trash folder where they remain—unless or until they are expunged.

I opened the trash folder. *Bingo!* The missing emails had been deleted but, fortunately, not expunged.

The first was an email sent by Ryan to his mother after Marie had moved from Rue des Écoles—the email Mrs. Song had told me about.

> I'm OK, Mom. Paris is cool. I'm seeing the sights with a girl named Meighan . . .

I had to agree with Mrs. Song that he didn't sound too shook up about Marie. I scanned further until I found one sent to Scooter dated February 24th—five days before Ryan died.

> Scooter, I know you and Brad have the answers to Professor Van's exams. That's not fair to the rest of us. Do the right thing, brah.

"Not fair to the rest of us" suggested that at this point only Scooter and Brad had the exams, which was corroborated by Van's grade sheet. I checked Ryan's inbox for an answer from Scooter. None. But I found one from Brad dated February 26th.

> If you know what's good for you, Ryan, you'll mind your own fucking business.

I looked for more emails between Ryan and the two guys, but found none. If the battle of words had escalated, it must have been through verbal exchanges rather than emails.

Next I checked Ryan's laptop for documents. If the suicide note had been printed from his computer, the document still might be there. But I couldn't find it, of course. Until I clicked the trash icon on his desktop. There it was: Au Revoir, Marie

The document had been created on March 1ˢᵗ at 2:13 am, Paris time (to which the laptop was still set). That was several hours after Ryan reportedly died. He couldn't have printed the note himself. And whoever had trashed it afterwards had neglected to empty the trash.

No wonder the Paris police had failed to mention these documents in their report. They may have given Ryan's laptop a cursory look, but found nothing.

The emails and the suicide note provided circumstantial evidence that Ryan had been murdered because he threatened to expose cheating in Van's history class. That the cheating had become more widespread, involving every student except Ryan, meant all had a motive to cover up. What I needed was specifics—who did what and when. What I needed was somebody to talk. I didn't expect Brad or Scooter would implicate themselves. And I didn't expect Heather would let Kim talk to me again. With Marie accessible only by email, that left Meighan.

Serena had given me her address: the Marco Polo, a once swanky seventies-era condo on Kapiolani Boulevard overlooking the Ala Wai Canal and Waikīkī. I drove there hoping to find her at home.

It was late. You can't get into the Marco Polo at night without a pass card, so I followed a resident in. Meighan lived on the 27ᵗʰ floor, in a studio apartment facing the mountains, rather than the water. I knocked. The blonde opened and didn't look surprised to see me.

"Meighan, I know now Ryan was murdered," I said. "I'm here to give you one last chance to clear yourself. Some of your classmates already have."

She didn't even blink. "Come inside."

Meighan led me into her tiny studio apartment. We sat on the edge of her bed, which also served as a couch.

"Tell me everything," I said. "And don't leave anything out this time."

"Okay, I was telling you the truth when I said I found Ryan hanging in his room naked. I couldn't believe he'd do that."

"He didn't."

"I know he didn't, but I didn't know it then."

"When did you find out?"

"Later that morning. When Heather, Kim and I got Brad and Scooter, they all acted shocked, like I told you, but I could tell they were faking. They were saying phony stuff like, 'Oh, it's so sad.' None of it seemed real."

"What happened next?"

"I finally said 'I don't believe this. Ryan wouldn't hang himself.' Then Brad snarled, 'You better shut your face. You're involved as much as we are.' Brad could get violent when he was angry. I'd already seen that."

"What did you see?"

"About a week before, Heather came to class one day with a black eye. She said she fell on the stairs. We all knew she was sleeping with Brad and we all figured he just went off on her, for whatever reason."

"She didn't confide in you or Kim about it?"

"Not me. Maybe Kim," Meighan said. "But Heather usually defended Brad—made excuses for him. You know how it goes."

"Unfortunately," I said, "the cycle of domestic abuse."

"Anyway, that's why I was scared of him," Meighan confessed. "That's why I went along when he said we all had to stick together. He said if Ryan's death looked suspicious, the cheating might come out. If it did, Brad might not graduate and his rich dad would cut him off. Brad was freaked about that."

"Did you already have the exam answers when Ryan died?"

She bowed her head and lowered her voice. *"Yes.* They gave them to me a few days before. But I didn't use them——"

"Until afterwards." I completed her sentence.

She nodded slowly. Her eyes moistened.

"Why did you cheat? Aren't you on scholarship?"

"That's just it. I have to maintain an A-minus average to keep my scholarship. I wanted to have fun in Paris and I thought— *stupidly*—that the answers would give me a little more time. I had no idea any harm would come to Ryan. Honest!"

"How did harm come to him?"

"When he found out Scooter and Brad had the exam answers and wouldn't stop cheating, Ryan told the rest of us. Then Heather went straight to Brad."

"Brad wasn't sharing the exams with her already?"

"I don't think so," Meighan said. "But he gave them to her then. And to Kim and to everyone else."

"To Ryan?"

"He tried, but Ryan wouldn't take them."

"Who hanged him?"

"I never asked. It was too horrible. And too stupid. Ryan was hanging there naked. So unlike him. That's why I slipped the board shorts on him—before I knew what really happened. Later Heather put the photo of Marie under him. And Kim typed the suicide note on Ryan's laptop. She didn't know much French, but she did know *au revoir.*"

"Was Marie involved?"

"No. She still thinks Ryan hanged himself. And she still feels guilty. Like it was her fault—because she moved in with Pierre."

"Then why did Marie cheat?"

Meighan looked surprised. "How'd you find out?"

"We detectives have our ways," I said. "Anyhow, wasn't Marie a brilliant student?"

"Yes, but when she moved in with Pierre she sort of flipped. She'd never been off the island before and she'd never had a lover. Suddenly she's living in Paris with a French guy. All she wanted was to spend time with him. She let her coursework slip. Being with Pierre was more important to her than anything."

sixteen

The next day I called Professor Van and told him I knew Ryan Song had complained to him about cheating in his history course. And I knew that Van had concealed this information from the Paris Police, from Paradise College, and from me. I asked him why.

"Are you going public with this?" he asked.

"Depends," I said.

"Ryan is dead," he replied. "That can't be changed."

"But you might have saved his life. I guess you were more concerned about your reputation—about how it might look if so many of your students got caught cheating."

"Ryan brought me accusations, not proof."

"I saw your grade record, Professor," I said.

Van was quiet.

"A scandal like this," I said, "and you could kiss the Hilo Hattie Chair goodbye."

"Are you going public?" he asked again.

seventeen

I called Scooter's cell phone after talking to Van and asked if I could see him one last time to wrap up my investigation. I could barely hear him over the blare of hip-hop music, but he said, "Didn't find anything, eh?"

"How'd you guess?" I replied.

"Too bad, man!" He sounded pleased, rather than sorry. "I'm at the Z Lounge. Brad's with me."

"Hang on," I said. "I'll be there in fifteen."

"Uh, we'll hang on. We're not going anywhere."

I hopped in my car and was there in less than ten. The Z Lounge was a hostess bar and strip joint on a seedy block of Kona Street. The odor of stale beer and cigarettes hit me as I stepped into the darkness. Hip-hop blared. You can't smoke there anymore, but before the law was changed the dark paneled walls got saturated. The proprietor, a former Madame named Michi, knew how to keep customers coming with exotic dancers and happy hour specials. It was too early for either, so there weren't any customers except Brad and Scooter who sat alone at the bar with their beers. Take that back—a young woman from the establishment had her arm around Brad and a drink in front of her.

I took the stool next to Scooter and ordered a beer. He turned to me.

"So you're wrapping up, huh?" he asked.

"You bet," I replied.

"Don't tell Heather." Brad gestured to the woman with her arm around him and winked.

"My lips are sealed," I said.

"We feel really sorry for Ryan's parents," Brad continued, "but they should have saved their money. Oh well, at least you got a gig."

"That I did," I said.

"So what's left to wrap up?" Scooter asked.

"Oh, I just wondered who put the rope around his neck." I sipped my beer. "Was it you or Brad?"

"Huh?" Scooter clinked his bottled on the bar. "What are you talking about?"

"Ryan," I said, "which one of you handled the rope?'

"Hey, man," Brad said in a menacing tone, "can't you see there's a lady present?" She smiled. "Anyway," he continued, "Ryan committed suicide."

"He didn't," I said.

"He didn't?" Scooter put on a dumb look.

"You guys had it all planned. But what you didn't plan on was somebody talking. Or somebody checking Ryan's laptop."

"This is bullshit, man!" Brad fumed. "What do you think you're doing, coming in here and saying this kind of crap to us? Do you think you're funny? Or are you just a complete asshole?"

"Point is, Brad, you and Scooter hung Ryan because he found out you had answers to Professor Van's exams. First you tried to shut him up by threatening him and then by giving him the answers. But that didn't work because Ryan wouldn't take them. He refused to cheat. That pissed you off even more. And it put you in jeopardy—because if Ryan told Van, you two would flunk the course and not graduate. And if you didn't graduate, Brad, your dad would cut you off. So you cooked up a scheme to make Ryan's murder look like suicide. You coerced Kim and Heather and Meighan into helping and kept them quiet by threatening to implicate them if they talked. It was a halfway decent plan. And it worked—for a while."

Brad and Scooter glanced at each other. I put a five on the bar, stood, and turned toward the door.

"So what happens now?" Scooter looked bewildered.

"Did you guys like France?" I said.

"Yeah," he replied. "It was cool. Why?"

"Because that's where you'll probably do your time."

I stepped from the reek and darkness into the afternoon sun.

eighteen

When I crossed Kona Street and walked to my car, I heard my name called from behind. It was Scooter, pushing opening the door of the Z Lounge and following me. He jogged across the street and came toward me. Instinctively I popped open the trunk and retrieved my Smith & Wesson—in case Scooter got nasty.

"Kai, wait," Scooter stopped a few feet from me. He didn't look angry. Just kind of confused. "You've got it wrong."

"Got what wrong?" I stood by my open trunk, gripping the revolver. "You guys are going down for what you did."

"I didn't do it," he said. "It wasn't me in Ryan's room with Brad. It was Heather. *She* put the rope around his neck."

"Who are you trying to kid?" I said, dumbfounded at his stupidity. "Heather was at the pharmacy, complaining of a sore tummy. But actually she's pregnant, if you don't already know."

"I knew she was pregnant. We all knew. But she wasn't at the pharmacy when Ryan died—like she told Kim and everyone else. The pharmacy on Rue des Écoles closes at eight. She was in Ryan's room with Brad. She went to talk with Ryan and asked Brad to go with her, because she was scared about getting caught cheating. They didn't intend to kill Ryan at first. Just to talk. But Brad got pissed off, like he always does, and knocked Ryan down. His head hit the floor really hard. They didn't wait to find out if he was passed out or dead. The got a rope from the utility closet, stripped off his clothes, and strung him up. They hung him naked over a photo of Marie to make it look like he killed himself because of her."

"Where were you when all this was happening?" I asked, my question inadvertently lending credibility to his story.

"Asleep in my room. I'd had a few too many already that night and was sleeping it off."

"*Right,*" I said.

"It's the truth, man!" Scooter insisted.

I almost believed him, but said, "It will all get sorted out back in Paris. Better pack your bags."

He turned, looking dejected, and walked back to the Z Lounge. Before he got there, the door swung open again. It was Brad. He waited for his friend to reach the door and then punched him in the face. Scooter didn't go down. He swung back. Before long it was a brawl. Michi came out and screamed. Then she flipped open her cell phone.

No honor among thieves . . . or murderers, I thought as I watched the brawl unfold. Then I heard sirens and saw two HPD cruisers pull up in front of the lounge. Before long the brawl was over and each man was inside a cruiser.

I followed the cruisers to police headquarters on Beretania Street. When the officers unloaded Brad and Scooter, I would be there. And then I'd catch up with my old pal Fernandez in homicide.

On the way to the station I remembered Meighan telling me Scooter looked like he'd been drinking the night Ryan died. Then I became more convinced Scooter was telling the truth. And I kicked myself for not checking out Kim's story that Heather had gone to the pharmacy that night. An internet search could have easily pulled up addresses and hours of pharmacies near 44 Rue de Écoles.

The case was not about the two buddies ganging up on Ryan. I had missed some subtle clues. But I'd put the big pieces of the puzzle together. Soon all the little pieces would fall into place too.

epilogue

I wish this case had a happier ending. My finding the killers of Ryan Song did not bring him back to his grieving parents. But the torment left their faces when I told them their son did not take his own life—that he had paid with his life for standing up for what he believed in. I assured them that his heartless killers would be brought to justice.

I met with the Songs over a quiet dinner at their St. Louis Drive home. During the meal they thanked me.

"When we heard about you from the college," Mrs. Song said, "we knew that if anyone could prove Ryan didn't take his own life, it was you."

I thanked them for their confidence in me.

But what especially pleased me was the change in Mr. Song. When he rose from the table to say goodbye, he stood erect with a look of self-assurance in his eyes. He smiled through his pain with a smile that seemed to come from deep within his heart. Nothing could ever compensate for his loss, but he was no longer a broken man. His pride in his son, and himself and his family, had returned.

Mrs. Song stood at his side when I bid them *aloha*. She too managed a faint smile as she waved goodbye.

About the Author

Chip Hughes learned to surf in San Diego in the late 1960s. He earned a Ph.D. in English at Indiana University and taught American literature, film, writing, and popular fiction for nearly thirty years at the University of Hawai'i at Mānoa. His non-fiction publications include two books on John Steinbeck and numerous essays and reviews.

An active member of the Private Eye Writers of America, he launched the Surfing Detective mystery series in 2004 with *Murder on Moloka'i*. The second book, *Wipeout!*, followed in 2007. The third, *Kula,* in 2011. Other titles, in various stages of development, are underway. The series is published exclusively by Slate Ridge Press. More at http://surfingdetective.com.

Hughes lives in Windward O'ahu with his wife, Charlene, and two retrievers. He still surfs when time allows.

Made in the USA
Coppell, TX
26 October 2019